KT-383-650

Please return/renew this item by the
last date shown to avoid a charge.
Books may also be renewed by phone
and Internet. May not be renewed if
required by another reader.

www.libraries.barnet.gov.uk

LONDON BOROUGH

*For my thoughtful, patient (not to mention handsome!)
husband, Todd Patrick Coletto, who knows that when I'm
writing and say I need "just five more minutes", I really
mean "forty-five" – and who loves me anyway.*

J.K.

For Louise, thanks for all your support.

C.J.

First published 2021 by Walker Books Ltd
87 Vauxhall Walk, London SE11 5HJ

2 4 6 8 10 9 7 5 3 1

Text © 2021 Amanda Kopy Jordan
Illustrations © 2021 Chris Jevons

The right of Jordan Kopy and Chris Jevons to be identified as author
and illustrator respectively of this work has been asserted by them
in accordance with the Copyright, Designs and Patents Act 1988

This book has been typeset in Berkeley Oldstyle Book

Printed and bound by CPI Group (UK) Ltd, Croydon CR0 4YY

British Library Cataloguing in Publication Data:
a catalogue record for this book is available from the British Library

ISBN 978-1-4063-9262-3

www.walker.co.uk

THEODORA HENDRIX
and the Curious Case of the
CURSED BEETLE

JORDAN KOPY

illustrated by Chris Jevons

WALKER
BOOKS

MONSTROUS LEAGUE of MONSTERS
CHARTER

1. Keep monsters hidden from humans
2. Protect humans from bad monsters
3. Help bad monsters become good monsters

PROLOGUE

Top-Secret Information

You there – *yes*, you. Are you alone? Good, because what I'm about to share is privileged – no, classified – no, top-secret information; not even the Queen of England or the President of the United States knows what I'm now going to tell you.

But perhaps I shouldn't. I don't need you blabbing to your parents or your teacher or your coach who's convinced you're the next big footie star and who makes you run laps until it feels like your legs are going to fall off and your lungs are going to explode.

They won't be pleased; I've already said too much.

The last time we met, I told you a secret, the biggest secret there ever was: the world is full of monsters. Good monsters, bad monsters, monsters who "forget" to comb their hair and brush their teeth… That isn't news to you, but *this* will be: we've received reports of some unusual monster activity deep in the deserts of Egypt. There, nestled between the shifting dunes of sand, in a village so small it has no name, a series of strange incidents have occurred.

One morning, the villagers awoke to find that their entire colony of well-loved strays had vanished, as if some giant, invisible hand had plucked all the dogs from the streets while they slept. That afternoon, they were even more dismayed to discover that their freshwater well had dried up; hordes of beetles now surged from its empty depths, spilling into the settlement in hissing black waves. And that night, when the moon hung low in the starless sky, they heard a strange scraping sound, as if something big and heavy was being dragged past their windows. No one dared to get out of bed to look, but in the morning they found tracks running the length of the dusty road.

Of course, the villagers didn't know that beneath their feet, miles below the sand, someone had broken into an ancient, long-forgotten tomb, stealing not one, not two, but six sarcophagi. It was the tomb of a creature so fearsome and formidable that even the brave members of the Monstrous League of Monsters (the MLM for short) avoided speaking its name, referring to it only as the Beetle King.

It goes without saying that the London branch of the MLM had bigger fish to fry than some far-flung, far-off evil. A fish by the name of Inspector Mary Shelley, who would soon be arriving on their doorstep.

Just one inhabitant – incidentally, the only human inhabitant – of the MLM mansion was unconcerned: Theodora Hendrix, who honestly didn't see what all the fuss was about. After all, she'd just faced down an evil hag who wanted to keep her as a pet, a thieving, skiving skele-crow and an army of the undead – how bad could an inspector be?

Pretty bad, as it turns out.

Now, I'm sure you're wondering what any of this has got to do with you? That's for me to know and for you to find out, Agent-in-Training. For now, let's just say we're building a case.

Agent Charles Holmes,
Eye Spy Monster Agency

The Head of Anubis

It was a dreary sort of day, the kind made for dozing on the couch. (Did your parents say the park is closed? It's not. They're just too lazy to take you. Not that I would ever call your parents lazy…) And that's exactly what the residents of Appleton, England, were doing in their cosy little homes: napping. But there was one house that was anything but sleepy; in fact, today it was downright lively.

Sprawling, peeling and crumbling like a cookie, this particular house – or I should say, mansion – did nothing to endear itself to the neighbours.

"I saw a spider as big as a hubcap walking up the front path, cool as you please," said Mrs Next Door, eyeing the cobweb-shrouded door with a shudder.

"That's nothing," replied Mrs Across the Street. "Yesterday, a statue – ugly thing with horns – fell right off the roof." She didn't mention that she'd distinctly heard it say, "That's the last time I let Bob help me fix the chimney." (The amount of energy grown-ups spend pretending that monsters don't exist is truly astonishing.)

"Makes you wonder what kind of people would live there," Mr Down the Road added.

Of course, people wouldn't – and didn't – live there; the members of the London MLM did. And at that very moment, they (unlike their nosy neighbours) were very busy indeed.

In the kitchen, Wilhelmina, the resident witch, was sweating over a cauldron, the contents of which smelled faintly of sage.

In the attic, the
operatic ghost,
Figaro, was practising
his scales to the dulcet
tones of a xylophone
made of crocodile
teeth. In the tallest tower,
Dracula, that most infamous
vampire, was pacing beneath a
fluttering cloud of bats, a letter bearing
the initials HQ clutched in his cold, bloodless
hands. But it is in the
Ancient Curse
Breaking Room
that our story
begins.

The Ancient
Curse Breaking
Room was rather
spooky, even
for a haunted

mansion. The cavernous chamber called to mind a vast, gilded cave: the windowless walls were etched with Egyptian hieroglyphics and dotted with weapons, while dozens of painted sarcophagi lined the perimeter. A towering stone jaguar took up one corner, occasionally letting out a tremendous roar whenever he felt things were getting a bit too quiet. In another, Mummy the mummy was working at a desk made from the curved tusks of a woolly mammoth. Sitting beside her was a ten-year-old girl with grass-green eyes and curly red hair in want of brushing: Theodora Hendrix, of course.

Theodora was the reason the MLM was under investigation in the first place: when the monsters found her abandoned in a graveyard and adopted her some ten years previously, they'd broken Headquarters' **Rule Number One:** *Keep monsters hidden from humans.* They got away with it, too – until a hag named Hilda had threatened to reveal their secret. The London MLM had no choice but to take matters into their own hands and had reported themselves to Headquarters. Luckily, Headquarters hadn't punished them, reasoning that, while the monsters had broken the first rule, they had upheld **Rule Number Two:** *Protect humans from bad monsters.* However, they wanted to be certain that there was no pattern of rule-breaking – hence the inspector's imminent arrival.

At the moment, Theodora wasn't concerned about the inspector, nor her investigation; she was concerned about the scary – no, frightening – no, horror-fying – sight before her. (I suggest skipping ahead a few pages if you're squeamish.)

On the desk stood a clay figurine with the head of a jackal and the body of a man. It was twenty-five centimetres tall and its eyes were aglow, a stream of emerald smoke pouring from its mouth.

"Who dares to disturb me?" demanded the little statue.

The tiny hairs on the back of Theodora's neck stood on end; the figurine's mouth hadn't moved. Despite this, its voice was booming, as if ten voices were speaking instead of one.

"Who dares to disturb me?" the statue repeated menacingly.

Mummy straightened, carefully tucking a loose strand of bandage behind her ear. "It is I, Mummy. Begging your pardon, Anubis, but we're in need of your assistance."

"Mummy, hmm? What assistance do you seek?"

In reply, Mummy opened an intricately carved, velvet-lined box. From its depths she withdrew a dazzling string of jewels, the oversized stones clinking together like wine glasses. "These have just arrived. There was no note. We're going to examine them for magical properties, but first, can you please tell us if they've been tampered with, or cursed?"

Mummy took curses very seriously. The worst punishment Theodora had ever received was after she'd accidentally released one into the mansion. She'd been banned from the Ancient Curse Breaking Room ever since, unless she was with Mummy or another responsible monster. In effect, this meant she was only allowed in if she was with Mummy, because the others simply refused to enter.

"Meow!" Bandit, the masked vampire-cat, would tell his best friend Georgie, the zombie, whenever it came up. Now, I don't speak cat, but I think what he said must have been something along the lines of, "That room has too many weapons and not enough mice and I don't like it at all, not one little bit!"

"Eurg," Georgie would reply with a shudder.

"Mew?" Bandit would ask, meaning, "I don't understand why you don't like sarcophagi, Georgie. They're just like coffins and you love napping in those. Still, there's something creepy about that room – lately, I've had the feeling that I'm being watched, even when it's supposed to be empty..."

The friends would exchange uneasy glances,

tacitly agreeing to say no more about it.

Mummy, however, did not mind the abundance of weapons or the lack of mice and was wholly unbothered by the presence of sarcophagi, given that her own was amongst those in the chamber. Yes, she was perfectly at ease in the Ancient Curse Breaking Room – even when being ordered about by a tiny statue.

"Place it around my neck," Anubis commanded in his thunderous voice, causing Theodora to jump.

Of course, this was impossible, as the necklace was meant to be worn by a fully grown adult and not a small figurine. Mummy wisely didn't point this out, laying the jewels on the desk so that Anubis was positioned in the middle of the circle of gleaming stones.

There was a sudden bang, loud as a cannon. Mummy didn't bat an eyelid, but Theodora was so startled she slid right off her seat. Looking up, she was met by a rather alarming sight: Anubis's head was no longer attached to his body. It was upside

down, teeth clamped onto a fat, shimmering ruby.
With another bang, he flopped, head over neck,
onto a glittering sapphire. On he went, nibbling on
each of the stones as if tasting them. (Are you all
right? You look a bit queasy – you'll need to buck up
if you're going to make it as an agent.)

"It's not been tampered with," said the head of
Anubis, reattaching itself to its body with a final
bang. "And I don't think it's cursed – but you should
still test it, just to be sure."

"Perfect," said Mummy, relieved.

Anubis didn't reply. The light in his eyes had
vanished; he appeared to have gone to sleep.

"And now to examine the amulet," said Mummy.
"That's where you come in, Theodora."

"How?" she asked eagerly, dusting herself off.
Assisting Mummy in the Ancient Curse Breaking
Room was one of her favourite things to do; it made
her feel very grown-up indeed, being entrusted
with such important work. Of course, she suspected
that Mummy didn't really need her help (she'd
been breaking curses for thousands of years before
Theodora was even born), but even so, it was nice to
spend some time together, just the two of them.

"With this," said Mummy, smiling mysteriously
as she slid the desk drawer open. She withdrew an
object that resembled a magnifying glass: it had a
large, circular lens mounted onto a golden handle
dotted with hieroglyphics. The only difference, really,
was that the lens wasn't clear – there was something
inside it: a bright blue eyeball, identical to the one
the monsters used in place of a doorbell (good thing
Mrs Across the Street had never noticed *that*).

"It's a Sight Extender," Mummy explained,

passing it to Theodora. "Hold it over the necklace. If the eye turns red, then the artefact is cursed. If it turns yellow, it's not."

Theodora did as instructed, gripping the Sight Extender in both hands. After a moment, the eye glowed yellow, shining so brilliantly it looked as if she were holding a tiny sun.

"Thank darkness," said Mummy. "I was almost

sure it was cursed when I held it."

"Pardon, madam," called a deep, mournful voice from the doorway. It could only belong to Helter-Skelter, the mansion's skeletal butler. "Dracula has requested your presence in his tower."

Mummy frowned. "I'd better see what's going on," she said, placing the jewels and the Sight Extender back on the desk, one on top of the other. She stood, motioning for Theodora to do the same. "We'll finish this later, OK?"

As Theodora and Mummy hurried from the room, neither noticed that the Sight Extender was no longer glowing yellow, but burning an angry, vivid red…

But someone did.

Ms FRUMPLE SAYS:

Laughing is punishable by detention!

Policy Changes

Theodora awoke to the screech of her alarm clock. Bleary-eyed and pale (why did school have to start so early?), she rolled out of bed, taking care not to disturb Sherman, the talking tarantula, his tasselled nightcap fluttering in time to his snores. (I don't care how lovely or well-dressed the tarantula – I certainly wouldn't allow one to share my pillow.)

Theodora slipped on her favourite zombie-bunny slippers and padded into the bathroom. She washed her face, brushed her teeth and dragged a comb through her hair, though she regretted this at once: two of its pink plastic teeth broke off into her tangled curls. With a shrug, she returned to her

room and dressed for school.

"Oh, good," said Mummy,
popping her head in. "You're up. Breakfast?"

"Yes, please," Theodora replied. "I've just got to
do my reading first."

No, Theodora hadn't left her homework to the
last minute (not this time); she was referring to her
torat cards. As you'll recall, torat cards, like tarot
cards, offer insights into the reader's life. Indeed,
the two are similar, except for a few small – but
significant – differences.

Firstly, torat cards can only be read by the child
for whom they were made; if your snotty older sister
Beatrice or your belligerent Uncle Rupert tried to
read them, they wouldn't be able to – they would
just see a regular pack of playing cards. Secondly,
torat cards are created by the elusive rata-tat-
tats, fashionable ladies known for their oversized
sunglasses and bright red lipstick.

Recently, the torat cards had also revealed a
third, lifesaving attribute: they had mysteriously

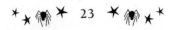

changed, their images altering to feature the skele-crow and the hag who'd tried to kidnap Theodora. Thanks in no small part to the cards' warnings, she'd managed to avoid this terrible fate. The deck had since reverted to its normal state, but Theodora was keeping an eye out for any new changes. With this in mind, she shuffled the cards and randomly selected three, placing them side by side on her bed.

The first card, which represented Theodora's past, featured a golden-haired woman dressed in flowing robes of powder blue.

"*The Lady*," she sighed, "as usual." No matter

 how often she shuffled the deck, Theodora always selected *The Lady*, which symbolized mysteries and secrets. She supposed this was fitting: to this very day, no one knew who her human parents were, why they'd abandoned her in a graveyard, or what had become of them since.

The second card, which represented Theodora's present, featured a man standing in a field of wildflowers stretching towards a cloudless, sun-drenched sky. He held a wand in one hand and a sword in the other.

"*The Magician,*" she said thoughtfully. "Trickery. Illusions. Deception."

The third and final card, which represented her future, depicted six black and white birds huddled together at the bottom, and a lone bird at the top.

"*The Seven of Magpies.* Thievery. Filching. Pilfering."

"Theodora," Mummy called from downstairs. "You're going to be late for school!"

"Coming!" Theodora sing-songed. She hurried down the hall, pausing at the top of a marvellous staircase inlaid with hundreds of human eyes. The ivory stairs, which had been rippling like waves a moment earlier (just one of the many quirks of 13 Battington Lane), stilled as she approached. She skipped down their length, jumping the last step just as Mummy rounded the corner.

"There you are," she said, handing Theodora her rucksack and a piece of buttered toast. "Bandit's waiting to take you to school. If you hurry, you might still make it on time. And, Theodora? Do try and behave. I have a feeling your head teacher is going to be keeping a close eye on you after that disaster with the school secretary –" we'll get to that in a minute – "and with Inspector Shelley arriving next week – well, it would be best for everyone if Ms Frumple wasn't poking around just now."

How very right Mummy was to warn her, for Ms Frumple had every intention of making trouble for Theodora. Lots of trouble.

Theodora was the last to reach her classroom. The rest of 5D were already seated, including her best (and only) human friend, Dexter Adebola. Small, slight and bespectacled, Dexter was the only person in all of Appleton who knew that Theodora lived with a family of monsters. He waved as she scurried between the desks, hoping to slip into her chair beside him unnoticed by their teacher, Mrs Dullson. Unfortunately, she had no such luck.

"You are very nearly late, Theodora," Mrs Dullson said without turning around. (I am convinced that teachers do, in fact, have eyes in the back of their heads.)

"Sorry, Mrs Dullson."

"I suggest you start making more of an effort to arrive on time," her teacher replied, depositing a marker onto the whiteboard ledge. "In future, the consequences for failing to do so will be severe: Ms Frumple has informed me of changes to the attendance policy, effective immediately."

Theodora's and Dexter's eyes met across their desks; this couldn't be good.

"Going forward, students who are late even once will receive a detention. Is that clear?" Her gaze swept across the room, touching briefly upon Theodora before settling on Billy Ellis, a boy with an unfortunate habit of picking his nose when he thought no one was looking.

"Yes, Mrs Dullson," the class chanted.

"Good, then I'd like you to copy the day's objectives off the board."

"W-what do you think a-about that?" Dexter

whispered, eyebrows wriggling like caterpillars.

"Typical Frumple," Theodora muttered. "Making up dumb rules just for the sake of it."

The room fell quiet except for the scratching of pens. A few minutes later, the silence was interrupted by a knock at the door.

"'Scuse me," said Mr Jackson, the school's crotchety old caretaker. "But the head teacher wants to see Theodora Hendrix straight away." He shuffled into the room, accompanied by his ever-present bucket and mop, and handed Mrs Dullson a crisp-looking note.

She unfolded the note, scanning its contents. "You'd better go, Theodora."

"But I didn't do anything!" Theodora said reflexively. (And for once, she really hadn't.)

"You'll have to take that up with Ms Frumple," Mrs Dullson said, not unkindly.

Theodora sighed. "Be right back," she muttered to Dexter, who looked as nervous as she felt. Pulse quickening, she followed Mr Jackson out of the room. "Did Ms Frumple say why she wants to see me?" she ventured to ask.

"Nope. Jus' that things are gonna be different round here from now on."

And on that ominous note he banged on the door to the head teacher's office.

The Return of the Most Villainous Villain

"Enter," called a muffled voice.

Mr Jackson opened the door. "In you get."

Wanting to get this over with as quickly as possible, Theodora straightened her hair ribbon, squared her shoulders and strode inside without further ado.

Most regrettably, the office looked nothing like it had when the former head teacher, Ms Sweet, occupied it: there were no photos of smiling classes past, no colourful student art hanging on the walls, no jar full of cookies sitting on the desk. It was plain and cold and sterile – which was fitting, because as far as Theodora could tell, Ms Frumple despised anything that most people considered fun.

And she was right: Ms Frumple did despise anything fun, and she absolutely loathed anything which she considered out of the ordinary. Perhaps this was why she'd taken an instant disliking to Theodora, who was rather unusual (I suspect this has something to do with growing up in a house full of monsters). Indeed, Ms Frumple was determined to rid Appleton Primary of anything – or anyone – that might be described as fun or out of the ordinary or unusual, including Theodora.

Theodora flung herself into the empty chair in front of Ms Frumple's desk. For a minute that lasted an hour (time doesn't fly when you're not having fun), the head teacher didn't speak. Instead, her gaze travelled over Theodora's slumped figure, lingering on the comb teeth still snarled in her hair. At last, she said, "I suppose you're wondering why I've called you here?"

Of course, she was very curious as to why the

head teacher wanted to see her, but she thought
it best to pretend otherwise: she was certain that
Ms Frumple would take any interest as a sign of
weakness and was determined not to give it to her.

"Ms Hendrix," the head teacher began, eyes
narrowing dangerously, "I have told you before that
I expect to be addressed as 'ma'am'. Do not give me
cause to remind you again."

"Yes, ma'am."

"You're aware of the changes made to the Appleton Primary attendance policy?"

"Yes. Mrs Dullson has just told us. Ma'am," she added, catching Ms Frumple's eye.

"Good, because that's what I want to discuss. You have an unfortunate habit of breaking school rules, Ms Hendrix." Before Theodora could object (as far as she was concerned, it was the rules which were unfortunate, not her habit of breaking them), Ms Frumple said, "But that ends today – unless you'd like me to recommend your immediate expulsion to the school governors, as I was inclined to do last week?"

Ms Frumple paused. Theodora was sure that she, too, was recalling the incident.

Theodora and Dexter had snuck out of class to meet Hilda at Appleton Cemetery. Theodora had intended to hand herself over in exchange for the hag's silence regarding the MLM's rule-breaking. But before Hilda could whisk her away, the MLM had appeared in all their monstrous glory. An earth-quaking, sky-cracking battle had ensued, concluding only when Theodora trapped Hilda in an empty grave – Georgie's grave, actually. The hag had then vanished, pulled underground by a hungry hobgoblin just as Ms Frumple arrived on the scene. The head teacher had promptly sought to expel the children for leaving the school grounds without the proper authorizations, but to her surprise – and then fury – permission slips for both students had suddenly appeared in the secretary's office, and the pair went unpunished.

"But as that happy day has been delayed," Ms Frumple continued softly, "I want to be sure that you and I understand one another."

Theodora straightened, Ms Frumple's tone putting her on alert (she had a finely tuned radar for such things, having spent many hours in the head teacher's office over the years).

"Things are changing around here, Ms Hendrix. The new attendance policy is just the tip of the iceberg. The school governors are considering additional modifications, including extending the school day, replacing Art with more academic subjects – and introducing uniforms, of course. Some of the students' current mode of dress is much too informal, not to mention unkempt," she added, eyeing Theodora's wrinkled shirt.

Theodora's face fell. Cancelling art? Extending the school day? It seemed Ms Frumple was determined to rid Appleton Primary of anything that made school remotely enjoyable. Her fists tightened at the thought.

A smirk slithered across Ms Frumple's face, as if she knew exactly what Theodora was thinking. "Any student who disrupts my efforts to improve this school will have to answer to me." She leaned forward until Theodora could see herself reflected in Ms Frumple's pale, glassy eyes. "And I will ensure that this student is expelled. Is that clear?"

"Crystal, ma'am."

"Then you may go."

Theodora didn't need telling twice; she was

on her feet before Ms Frumple had even finished speaking. She made her way back to class, thinking that Ms Frumple was, without a doubt, the worst thing to have ever happened to Appleton Primary; she was certainly the worst thing to have ever happened to her.

Of course, Theodora hadn't yet met Inspector Shelley.

Theodora wasted no time in filling Dexter in on all that had passed in Ms Frumple's office.

"S-she called you in j-just to give you a warning?" he asked, taking a bite of his ham and cheese sandwich. "That s-seems unfair."

"Since when has Frumple ever been fair?" Theodora said, popping a biscuit into her mouth. "I'm more worried about the changes she mentioned."

"M-maybe the school g-governors won't agree to them," Dexter said hopefully.

"Maybe," Theodora replied, unconvinced.

"Are you g-going to compete in next week's chess tournament?" he asked, changing the subject. Theodora didn't mind – any topic was better than their awful head teacher.

"Yeah!" she said with more enthusiasm than she felt; chess wasn't really her cup of tea. "Mummy's coming to watch. There's a PTA meeting after, so she needs to be here anyway."

I'm sure you're aware of this, but just in case you're not, PTA stands for Parent–Teacher Association. Basically, a group of concerned parents and long-suffering teachers get together to discuss all things student-related: fundraising for trips, organizing school discos and voting on whether or not the kitchen should stop serving unidentifiable lunch meat (the answer was always a resounding "yes", and yet, the ham remained indistinguishable from the turkey).

Why am I spending so much time talking about the PTA? Because the next meeting is going to be very important to our tale. (And how dare you question my storytelling abilities?!)

"Mummy's really nervous about the meeting," Theodora said. "They're supposed to vote on who's going to host this year's Halloween Fair – Mummy volunteers every year, but the other parents never vote for her."

"My mom will be t-there too. I'm sure she'll vote for Mummy. And my dad is g-going to try to make the chess tournament, so he'll also stay for the meeting – you know, if h-he can get away from work…"

"I'm sure he'll do his best," Theodora said encouragingly. Dexter's father, Mr Adebola, was a surgeon at a hospital in London. As he was very busy, he didn't always get to spend as much time with Dexter as either of them would have liked, and more often than not missed school functions.

The rest of the school day was uneventful. When the bell rang a few hours later, Theodora waved goodbye to Dexter and stepped into the playground, where she was nearly bowled – or perhaps I should say, blowed – over. The wind was raging something fierce, stinging her eyes and causing her hair to whip around her head. Bowing against the blustery gusts (was it normally this chilly in October?), Theodora staggered over to the school crossing.

"Hi," she said to the lollipop lady, wiping her leaky eyes with her sleeve. "Windy, isn't it?"

"Too right," the lollipop lady replied, raising her

sign to slow the incoming traffic. "Happened all of a sudden," she said abruptly. "There wasn't even a breeze a few minutes ago."

"How odd," Theodora replied.

Odd, indeed. Curious, even.

Housekeeping

It wasn't only the winds that were changing in
Appleton: a sudden chill had settled upon the village.
Gardens had frosted over, the frozen grass crunching
beneath the residents' boots as they went about their
business. At the MLM mansion, the pumpkins had
shrivelled (I shudder to think what Sir Pumpkin-
de-Patch, the Monster-Gardener-in-Chief, had to
say) and the cobwebs had hardened into icy veils,
glittering like diamonds in the late afternoon sun.

Neither Theodora nor Bandit (who'd been waiting
for her opposite the school) noticed any of this as they
made their way up the path to the mansion, eager as
they were to get out of the cold. Before Theodora's
freezing fingers could manage to unlock the front

door, it swung open with a familiar wail (not unlike that of a wounded animal, or your mum "singing" along to the radio). Bandit streaked inside without a backward glance, vanishing into the warmth.

"Come in," said Helter-Skelter, stepping aside to allow her to pass. "It's turned chilly. I've lit a fire in the Beelzebub Parlour if you'd like to warm up a trifle," he added, hanging up her jacket in the hallway, where one of the fox stoles – still very much alive and curled around a hanger – yawned widely.

"That's OK. I'm going to grab a snack from the kitchen," Theodora told the skeletal butler.

"Are you sure you wouldn't be more comfortable in the parlour?"

"Yes, there's leftover pizza in the fridge. I've been looking forward to it all day!"

"I can bring you a slice in the parlour," Helter-Skelter insisted, blocking her path.

Theodora frowned, unsure what to make of the butler's odd behaviour. Why didn't he want her to go into the kitchen? Before she could ask, Bon the bonadoo (a creature with the body of a hare and the teeth, mane and tail of a lion) hopped – yes, hopped – into the foyer.

"She's gone mad, Mummy has!" he cried. "You'd think the Monster Prime Minister was coming to stay, the way she's acting!" He shook his head, ears flapping against his golden mane. "She's got Georgie sweeping and Dracula scrubbing and poor Sherman's been spinning fresh webs for hours. But Mummy's out of her bandages," he added, thumping his foot for emphasis, "if she thinks I'm going to straighten up my den for the likes of that dragon!"

And with that he leapt out of sight, nose sticking up in the air.

"Why's Mummy making everyone clean up?" Theodora asked.

Helter-Skelter opened his mouth – or rather, jaw

– to reply, but at that moment Mummy herself came thundering into the hall, her expression so fierce Theodora half expected lightning bolts to shoot from her eyes.

"Helter-Skelter, where have you been?" she cried. "I've been looking for you everywhere. We've got to finish preparing tonight's supper; everything's got to be perfect. I seem to remember that sautéed fish eyes are her favourite – the chewier, the better. Do we have any? Yes? Good, then let's add them to the menu. Oh, there's no time to waste!"

"Right away, Mummy." Helter-Skelter bowed. "And remember, Theodora," he said in an undertone, "I tried to warn you."

"I'll ask Figaro to sing for the entertainment," Mummy muttered, seemingly oblivious to Theodora's presence, "and Dracula can perform his bat formations..."

Theodora frowned. It was unlike Mummy to be so distracted – and she'd never seen her looking so untidy: her wrappings were dishevelled and her crown was askew. "Mummy," she asked tentatively, "what's going on?"

Mummy blinked. "Theodora, when did you get home? And Sherman can explain," she said vaguely, heading towards the kitchen. "I've just sent him to your room to tidy up."

"What about my pizza?"

"After you've done your chores!" Mummy called; there was clearly to be no discussion.

Theodora trudged upstairs, her belly pizza-less. She came to an abrupt stop at the top of the staircase, mouth hanging open like a freshly caught carp's: she'd never seen the Great Hall looking so – well – clean. The rugs had been vacuumed, the candelabras dusted and dressed in fresh skeins of soft, fluffy cobwebs, and the suits of armour had been buffed to a high shine.

"Helter-Skelter rubbed me raw, he did," winced one of the suits, gingerly touching his visor.

"But why?" Theodora asked.

"Cursed if I know." The suit shrugged. "Didn't ask. Don't look at me like that – you wouldn't have, either, with Mummy in such a state."

Theodora threw him a baleful look as she strolled past.

"I've patched the drapes in the Mephistopheles Parlour," Sherman said by way of greeting, propelling himself down from the ceiling on a strand of spider silk. "They're still a little ragged along the seams, but it was the best I could do at short notice."

"Never mind the curtains!" Theodora snapped. "What in darkness' name is going on? Helter-Skelter wanted me to hide in the Beelzebub Parlour, Mummy's unravelling – literally – and the mansion is so clean its unrecognizable. The suits of armour aren't even creaking!"

"Haven't you heard?" Sherman asked maddeningly, peering at her through his many monocles.

"Heard what?" Theodora cried, stamping her foot in superb imitation of Bon.

"Inspector Shelley is arriving tonight, instead of next week."

"So?"

"So, if things aren't up to her standards – in other words, if they aren't absolutely perfect – Headquarters might reverse their Not Guilty verdict and punish us for breaking **Rule Number One**. And if they do, the MLM – including me – will be jailed in the darkest, dankest prisons of Transylvania, and you'll be sent to live with humans."

Theodora paled. "But I thought the verdict could only be reversed if the inspector finds proof of additional rule-breaking?"

"Yes, well…" Sherman said delicately, adjusting a monocle. "What Headquarters says it's going to do and what it actually does isn't always the same thing."

"But – but," Theodora paused, struggling to put her feelings into words. "That's not fair!"

"No," he agreed. "Which is why it's imperative that we give every appearance of proper monster behaviour. Now, Mummy's left us a list of chores," he said, tapping a long, hairy leg against a Post-it covered with Mummy's scribbled handwriting.

Theodora picked up the list, which read:

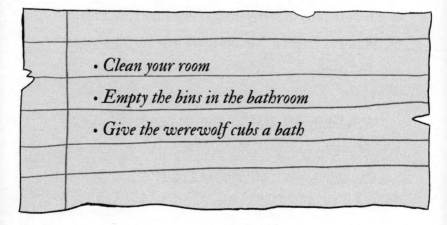

- *Clean your room*
- *Empty the bins in the bathroom*
- *Give the werewolf cubs a bath*

"This is going to take all night," she sighed.

"Better not," Sherman said in alarm. "Mummy won't be pleased if we haven't finished by the time the inspector arrives."

"I'm exhausted," Sherman moaned two hours later. He was lying on Theodora's bed, his many legs curled in on his stubby body – all except one, which was flung over his eyes.

"Me too," Theodora agreed, collapsing onto the bed beside him. But before her head had even hit the pillow, a harassed-looking Wilhelmina barged into the room.

"You're not dressed!" she cried.

"We've only just finished our chores," Theodora said defensively.

"Mummy wants you downstairs, NOW."

"But—"

"No buts! I suggest you put on something smart – maybe the frock with the lace collar and your best cemetery shoes – and meet us in the Beelzebub Parlour directly. You too, Sherman."

"That dress is too small," said Theodora, not at all sorry for it (she wasn't a fan of lace).

"No matter," Wilhelmina replied, withdrawing her wand from her pocket. She tapped it against her chin, sparks spouting from the tip. "Yes, that will do nicely. Alderdon-pallderdon!"

Theodora felt something whoosh over her head.

"That's better," Wilhelmina said, looking pleased.

Glancing down, Theodora saw that she was now wearing a red tartan dress and a matching hair ribbon. Sherman was sporting a fresh top hat.

"Thanks!"

"You're welcome," Wilhelmina replied, leading them out of the room. "Now, you're to be on your best behaviour."

"We know," sighed Theodora.

"I've had the displeasure of meeting Inspector Shelley before, and she's about as warm and cuddly as a frozen cactus. Back when I was stationed at the Salem MLM, she shut us down within a week of her arrival – said we hadn't properly protected the humans of Massachusetts during the Witch Trials some *two hundred* years earlier."

"That seems most unreasonable," Sherman sympathized.

"Unreasonable just about sums her up. There can be absolutely no rule-breaking in the inspector's presence."

"We knoooow," Theodora said again.

"Because if there is, there will be 'H, E, double-hockey sticks' to pay." The witch paused, levelling a severe look between them. "Headquarters won't hesitate to close our doors on her say-so. And if they do, the members of the London MLM will be reassigned to other agencies – if we manage to stay out of jail, that is – and you, Theodora, will be sent to live with—"

"Humans," Theodora finished, a knot forming in the pit of her stomach.

"Exactly," Wilhelmina nodded as they entered the parlour.

It, too, had undergone a rigorous cleaning: the ceiling was dusted, the sofa cushions freshly plumped and a fire crackled merrily in the massive marble fireplace.

"Ah, Theodora. Why don't you sit on the far settee?" suggested Dracula, who was dressed in his best satin-lined cape. "No point in hiding you. Inspector Shelley knows you're here, obviously. But I don't think it's wise to parade you about, either. What do you think, Mummy?"

"That's fine," said Mummy, offering Theodora a reassuring smile.

Theodora grinned, relieved to see that Mummy had straightened her tiara and put on a fresh set of bandages; not a single jewel or ribbon was out of place. The knot in Theodora's stomach loosened slightly. Mummy wouldn't let anything bad happen to her; she loved her too much. All her earlier fussing was just to make sure that things went as smoothly as possible with the inspector, for which Theodora was very grateful indeed.

From his perch on the mantle, Grimeny Cricket, the buggy bringer of death, asked, "When's the inspector due to arrive?"

As if in reply, there was a knock at the door.

The Inspector

"Places, everyone!" Dracula called in a stage whisper.

The monsters scattered.

"Welcome," they heard Helter-Skelter say from the hall. "May I take your coat?"

A few seconds later, a haughty-looking woman in a long black dress swept into the parlour. Theodora's first thought was that she looked as if she'd stepped out of the Victorian era (for those of you sleeping through History lessons, that's the period ranging from the mid to late 1800s) and strangely human – there didn't seem to be anything monstrous about her. Her second thought was that the inspector's narrow, pointed features called to mind a rat, but that might have been because an actual rat was poking its head out of her collar.

"Ah, the illustrious London MLM," the rat said in a silky voice. "The vampire's the head, though I've heard it's the mummy who really runs the show."

Dracula bristled at this, but the rodent paid him no mind. "The witch is powerful. I wouldn't worry about the cat or the zombie."

Bandit hissed in reply, but the rat ignored him, too.

"The werewolf has a temper," he added, gazing appraisingly at Marty. "I can tell by the way he's baring his teeth at me."

58

"That's enough, Ratsputin," said the inspector, her tone so icy it sent a shiver down Theodora's spine.

The rat fell silent. The monsters exchanged uneasy glances.

"And there's the child," Ratsputin burst out, seemingly unable to contain himself. "Odd-looking creature. Can't imagine why anyone would want to keep one."

"I said, that's enough," the inspector snapped.

The rat fell silent once more, though his beady, clever gaze did not waver from Theodora's face. She shifted uncomfortably in her seat, wishing he would look away.

"Erm, yes," Dracula began. "Inspector Shelley, welcome to the London MLM. We do hope you'll make yourself at home."

"I plan to," said the inspector, wandering over to the nearest window. "Who chose these curtains?" she murmured, fingering the heavy material. "This shade of red went out of style in 1882…"

"So tacky," the rat agreed, not bothering to keep his voice down.

Dracula glanced at Mummy, who had chosen the curtains and who looked slightly taken aback by their guests' rudeness.

"Would you like a tour?" Mummy offered, recovering herself. "Or would you prefer a rest before dinner?"

"Helter-Skelter has prepared quite a spread," Dracula added. "And we've got some wonderful entertainment planned – I myself will be performing—"

"A tour, I think," Inspector Shelley cut in. "The butler may accompany me."

And with that she strode from the room. Theodora shivered again as she passed; she could have sworn a few snowflakes fluttered to the floor in the inspector's wake.

If Theodora had harboured any hope that Inspector Shelley was not as awful as she first appeared, I'm afraid she was in for a rather rude awakening.

The very next morning, she was unceremoniously woken up at 6 a.m. by a loud banging at her door. "Go away," she muttered sleepily, burrowing deeper into the covers.

"Excuse me?" came Inspector Shelley's snooty voice.

Theodora's eyes popped open. The inspector! What was she doing outside her room? "Sherman," she whispered, jostling the still-snoring tarantula. "The inspector's here!"

"W-w-what?" he asked, yawning hugely.

"We don't have all day, you know," Ratsputin called through the door.

All eight of Sherman's eyes blinked open. Now fully awake, the tarantula hastily scuttled up Theodora's arm, settling on her shoulder as she scrambled to open the door.

"We're inspecting every room in the mansion

for signs of rule-breaking," Inspector Shelley began without preamble.

"A-at this time?" said Sherman, popping a monocle over his eye.

Ratsputin, still nestled in the inspector's collar, rose to his full height of twenty centimetres. "The inspector is a very busy monster and does not have time to waste, as you seem to do."

"These will have to go," Inspector Shelley said as she swept into the room, eyeing the scruffy comic-book posters that were hanging over Theodora's bed.

"Definitely," Ratsputin agreed. "Maybe we could put up some mirrors instead?"

Theodora glanced at Sherman, who merely shrugged; what Theodora's décor had to do with investigating the MLM for rule-breaking wasn't any clearer to him than it was to her.

With a last look at the inspector (now on her hands and knees, clutching a tape measure in her fist), they left her to it. They moseyed on down

to the kitchen, where Helter-Skelter was already
bustling about making breakfast.

"Theodora, Sherman," he said, placing a steaming
mug of tea in front of Mummy, who was seated at
the counter. "What are you doing up so early – and
at the weekend, no less?"

"Inspector Shelley is examining our room for

signs of rule-breaking," Theodora said grumpily, settling on a stool.

Mummy glanced up from her paper, *The Morning Monster Gazette*. "At this hour?"

"That's what I said," Sherman murmured.

"The inspector's wasted no time settling in," said Helter-Skelter, cracking two eggs into a sizzling pan. "Not only did she demand 'the best room in the mansion' – I've put her in the Macabre Suite – but she's already given me a list of her preferred foods and told me explicitly not to light any fires without her permission, nor to raise the thermostat

above four degrees Celsius.

"Is that why it's so cold in here?" Theodora shivered, wishing she'd grabbed her bathrobe.

"Yes," said Helter-Skelter, sliding a plate of eggs in front of her. "She's put signs about it everywhere, lest we forget and crank up the heat."

"I wish you would," said a windswept Wilhelmina, clutching a knobbly broom in her fist as she entered the kitchen. "She'd probably melt, and then we wouldn't have to put up with her. Here less than a day, and she's already proven herself to be a right pain in the—"

"How was your flight?" Mummy interrupted over Theodora's and Sherman's giggles.

Before Wilhelmina could respond, Sir Pumpkin-de-Patch tore into the kitchen. An odd-looking monster with a pumpkin for a head and a body made of vines twisted into the shape of a man, he looked even more peculiar today, wringing his hands and dropping leaves as he went.

"Mummy, I need you in the gardens at once!" he cried. "Those wretched trolls are throwing a party in the greenhouse – they've already broken several very expensive planters! And they—"

"Perhaps I was too hasty in promoting them to **Reform Level Three:** *Recognizing Bad Monster Behaviour*," Mummy mused, interrupting what promised to be one of the gardener's long-winded rants. "Don't worry," she added, putting down her paper as she slid off the stool. "We'll get it straightened out."

"Poor Sir Pumpkin-de-Patch," said Sherman as they exited the kitchen. "He was so proud of those planters – he had them made in Italy especially."

Theodora nodded absently. She was still thinking about Inspector Shelley. Why did the inspector like the cold so much? What kind of monster *was* she, anyway?

I must admit that I, too, am curious about this. Naturally, I have my suspicions, but perhaps we need to do a little more digging, just to be sure. Shall we?

The Hiding Place

In all the excitement, Theodora had forgotten to tell
Dexter not to come over on Saturday as planned
(Mummy had been quite clear that no humans –
present company excluded – were allowed at the
mansion until Inspector Shelley had vacated the
premises), and so at two o'clock sharp that afternoon
he rang the bell. Luckily, Helter-Skelter was there to
greet him, stealthily delivering Dexter to Theodora's
room without attracting anyone's notice.

"I told you Headquarters was sending an
investigator?" Theodora asked as Dexter settled
beside her and Sherman on the carpet, where they
had been reading a magazine, *Monsters Geographic*.

He nodded.

"Well, she came early. And let's just say she makes Ms Frumple look like a kind and sensitive woman."

"She's worse than Frumple?"

"Yup," Theodora said grimly. "All the monsters are talking about it. She's making everyone nervous, hinting at all the rules she's sure we're breaking. And she's really bossy, too, making us keep the thermostat at a certain temperature and telling us when we can eat our meals. Mummy said it's best if we just go along with it, but I can tell she isn't thrilled."

"And she's got this talking rat," Sherman added. "He's really—" he froze suddenly. "Someone's coming." (Tarantulas may have terrible eyesight, but they also have excellent hearing.)

"Dexter, you've got to hide, quick!"

But before Dexter could move so much as an inch the door swung open to reveal…

"Mummy," Theodora exhaled, though her relief was short-lived; Mummy did not look happy.

"Theodora, what on earth were you thinking, inviting Dexter over while the inspector's staying with us? Not that we aren't glad to see you, dear," she added to Dexter, who was blinking at the sight of Mummy dressed in her bandages instead of the twin set he was accustomed to seeing her in. (As you'll recall, monsters take a glamour potion to make themselves appear human when they go out in public.)

"I-I can ask my mom to p-pick me up?" Dexter offered.

"Now that you're here, you may as well stay. We'll bring you out right before your mum's supposed to collect you – you'll just have to stay out of sight until it's time to go."

Helter-Skelter appeared at Mummy's side. "Dracula has sent word that Inspector Shelley is headed this way," he said, nodding at the bat messenger hanging upside down from his bony finger. "She wants to interview the suits of armour…"

"That is not ideal." Mummy frowned; the suits were notorious gossips.

"Might I suggest moving the children to the music chamber, in case the inspector takes a detour?"

Mummy agreed that this was a good idea, and the little group made their way downstairs without incident – that is, until they heard an oily voice near by.

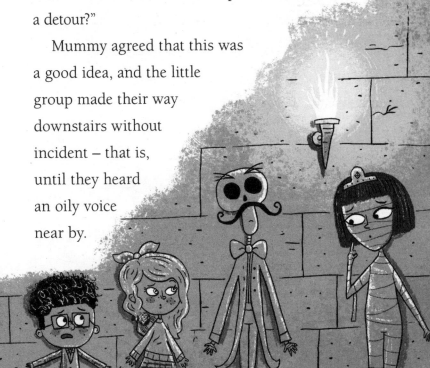

"Really, Dracula, who knew you were such a chatterbox? I thought vampires were supposed to be silent, mysterious types."

"Yes, well," they heard Dracula reply. "It's not every day the MLM receives such important visitors as yourselves. We're excited to show you what we've accomplished here."

"I suppose some might call hiding a human for ten years an accomplishment," Ratsputin said slyly.

"What should we do?" Sherman murmured, pincers clicking nervously.

"We can hide in here," said Theodora, darting towards the nearest door, which just so happened to belong to the Ancient Curse Breaking Room.

Mummy looked as if she were going to object, but at the sound of the rapidly approaching footsteps said, "Excellent idea." She opened the door, ushering the children and Sherman inside. "Stay still and DON'T TOUCH ANYTHING!" she hissed. The door closed behind them with a click, plunging the room into darkness.

"I d-don't like this," Dexter stammered.

"There's a light somewhere," Theodora said, dragging her hand along the wall until she found the switch. The torches roared to life, casting long, flickering shadows across the vast space.

"And I REALLY don't like this," Sherman fretted. "This room is haunted."

"The whole mansion is haunted," Theodora reminded him.

"There's haunted, and then there's haunted," muttered the spider.

"This place is huge," said Dexter, twisting his head towards the high, vaulted ceiling, the glittering walls, the towering statue of the jaguar. His gaze landed on the desk in the far corner of the room, where the sleeping statue of Anubis stood. "Th-Theodora," he said, pulling at her sleeve. "What's th-that?"

"That's Anubis."

"He's a good spirit," Sherman explained. "He occasionally enters that figurine to communicate

with Mummy when she calls – he's very loyal to her. He doesn't seem to be occupying it now, though."

"Not that," said Dexter, shaking his head. "That."

"Oh, that's a Sight Extender," Theodora said, leading him over to the desk. "Mummy and I were using it the other day to see if this necklace was cursed. Luckily, it wasn't."

And then something rather strange happened:

the Sight Extender blinked – or rather, the eyeball encased in it did.

At that moment, the door flew open with a bang. Theodora whipped around, seeking a place to hide. Her gaze landed on an unoccupied sarcophagus whose gilded edifice featured a vaguely familiar dark-haired woman with liquid-looking eyes. She hesitated. Dexter wasn't going to like it, but desperate times…

"In here," she said, dragging Dexter and Sherman into the casket before they could object. Soon the trio were immersed in darkness once more, though a little light seeped in through the slits where the mummy's eyes would sit. Theodora peered through one of the vents. A willowy figure filled the doorway, her voluminous skirts blowing about her legs despite the lack of wind.

Want to hazard a guess who?

Secrets, Secrets Are No Fun...

You're right, of course. It was Inspector Shelley.

"We'll take it from here, Dracula," she said, slamming the door in the vampire's face. She strode purposefully across the room, stopping barely half a metre from where the children were hiding. She immediately began to examine one of the other sarcophagi. Ratsputin scrabbled down her arm, leaping onto its lid. It was the first time Theodora had seen the rat outside of the inspector's collar. To her surprise, she saw that his tail wasn't pink and ribbed; it was green and scaly, snaking over his shoulder – probably because it was an actual snake.

"Inspector," Ratsputin said tentatively, "we checked this room last night. I'm afraid that Mummy's True

Name simply isn't here."

Theodora frowned. What was a "True Name" – and what did it have to do with Mummy?

"It's got to be here; we've looked everywhere else. You know what the legend says…"

"I do," the rat allowed. "But a legend is just that – a myth, a story. It's not necessarily true."

"And it's not necessarily untrue," the inspector countered.

"Yes, well … I still don't understand why we need Mummy's True Name in the first place."

Inspector Shelley skewered the rat with a steely glare. "We've been through this. I thought you, Ratsputin, with all your ambition, would understand: I wish to take over this household; I wish to be the new head of the London MLM."

Theodora gasped. Ratsputin's head swivelled in their direction, sniffing the air. She clasped a hand over her mouth as Dexter stiffened beside her; could the rat smell them? Theodora held her breath, releasing it only when he returned his attention to the inspector.

"And in order to do that," continued the inspector, "we need Mummy's help. We wouldn't stand a chance if we tried to take on the MLM by ourselves, but Mummy can easily overpower most monsters. And given how cosy they all are, I doubt the others will even raise their fists against her." Her lip curled in disgust, as if the fact that the monsters cared for one another was a bad thing. "She won't help us willingly, but if we learn Mummy's True Name, we can make her help us. And can you remember why that is?"

"Because if you have knowledge of a mummy's True Name, you can control that mummy's mind, forcing them to act however you please."

"Exactly. We'll use Mummy to take over the MLM, and then we'll be sitting pretty – no more blasted investigations for us! We'll finally be living the good life. I've always fancied living in a country mansion…"

"Working here is a rather cushy job," Ratsputin conceded. "And the mansion itself is fabulous. It needs some work, obviously, but I could live here."

"And we will," Inspector Shelley assured him, "just as soon as—" She broke off, turning as the door to the Ancient Curse Breaking Room opened once more.

"Inspector," Bon called from the doorway, unwilling to enter any further. "An urgent letter has arrived for you from Headquarters."

Inspector Shelley sighed impatiently, plucked Ratsputin off the sarcophagus and exited the room. Theodora waited a beat, then flung the coffin lid open.

She stumbled out, followed by a trembling Dexter.

"N-never again," he stuttered. "N-never, ever, again."

"There, there," Sherman said kindly, brushing himself down and straightening a monocle.

"Never mind that!" Theodora cried. "Did you hear what Inspector Shelley said? She's going to try to control Mummy's mind and use her to take over the MLM!"

"I heard," Sherman said heavily. "You're not going to like this," he sighed, glancing at Theodora, "but I think we've got to tell someone what we heard – a grown-up someone."

It was a mark of the seriousness of the situation that Theodora did not object; she simply nodded. "Follow me." She opened the door slowly, peering into the corridor to check that the coast was clear.

"Oh, good, I've caught you," Helter-Skelter said as they stepped into the hallway. "Dexter, your mother's here."

"That went fast! Thanks, I'll be right out. Are you guys going to be OK?" he added in a whisper to Theodora and Sherman.

"We'll be fine," Theodora whispered back. "I'll fill you in at school on Monday."

She and Sherman waved goodbye to Dexter and

continued down the corridor, coming to a halt in front of a door. Theodora knocked.

"Come in… Ah, Theodora, Sherman," said Dracula, looking up from his desk – a sprawling, gleaming mass of mahogany. "What a lovely surprise. What can I do for you?"

"We have a question," Theodora said. Up close, she could see dark smudges beneath the vampire's eyes, as if he'd dabbed charcoal on his skin.

Dracula smiled wanly, scribbling his signature on an official-looking document. "I hope I have an answer. Well?"

Theodora hesitated. Her gaze flitted to Sherman, who gave an encouraging nod. "What's a True Name?"

Dracula's hand jerked, splattering the parchment with ink. "How – where did you hear that term?" he sputtered.

"In the Ancient Curse Breaking Room."

The vampire's brows creased, forming a single, severe line. "Were you with Mummy?"

"Not exactly," Theodora hedged. "We were with Dexter … and Inspector Shelley."

At this, Dracula shot out of his seat. He strode across the study, pausing before a trolley proffering an array of blood-filled decanters. Dracula poured most of the contents of one glittering carafe into a glass and drank deeply. He refilled the glass, then returned to his seat.

"To answer your question, a 'True Name' is the name a mummy went by when he or she was human. Anubis is the Keeper of True Names," Dracula explained. "He takes them in exchange for allowing mummies to leave the Land of the Departed and to return to us here, in the Land of the Living."

"Is that why we call Mummy, 'Mummy' – because she gave Anubis her True Name?"

"Precisely."

"Inspector Shelley also said something about being able to control a mummy if you learn their True Name… Is that true?"

"I'm afraid so," Dracula said gravely. "Now, I want you to tell me exactly what happened." The shadows beneath his eyes deepened as Theodora, with Sherman's assistance, relayed all they had overhead. "In the name of all that's unholy," he said when they finished. "Are you quite sure you heard correctly?"

"We're sure."

"What a nightmare!" he cried, jumping to his feet. "And not the good kind!"

Theodora took an involuntary step back. She wasn't remotely afraid of Dracula, but in that moment, he looked so much the part of the bloodthirsty vampire – what with his fangs extending past his bottom lip, his dark, fathomless eyes dilated so she could no longer see their whites – that she understood, for the very first time, why most humans were.

"Inspector Shelley thinks she can run the MLM?" he ranted, beginning to pace. "How ridiculous – she doesn't have the experience! It's all very well to oversee investigations for Headquarters, but she has no idea what goes into managing an agency. She'd be putting millions of lives at risk – monster and human alike! No, she'll run this place over my undead body!" Dracula stopped suddenly, as if an idea had just occurred to him. He rifled through his desk, withdrawing a creased business card embossed with a drawing of an eye (or at least, what was supposed to be an eye; the sketch was rather lopsided).

Theodora gasped – she'd seen that card once before, in this very room…

"I need to make a call," Dracula said urgently, "and convene an emergency MLM meeting. In the meantime, I have a very important job for you two – if you're up to it?"

"We are," they said eagerly.

"I need you to distract Mummy; I don't want her to know that Inspector Shelley is searching for her True Name or about the emergency meeting. It could be a matter of life or death." The vampire spun on the spot, cape swirling in a swish of satin, and vanished, a dozen furry bats appearing in his place. "Do you understand?" they asked in their squeaky, high-pitched voices.

Theodora didn't, really; why didn't Dracula want Mummy to know what was going on – especially as it involved her directly? She was usually the first monster he went to at the slightest hint of trouble.

Before she could voice the question, the bats

said, "Once Mummy is sufficiently detained, come straight to the mausoleum."

"What sort of diversion can we create at such short notice?" Sherman wondered as the bats flitted off in a dozen different directions, presumably to gather up the members of the MLM.

A grin split Theodora's face. "I've got an idea."

... Unless They're Told to Everyone

I think this is a good time to debrief. Building a case requires a lot of detective work – and, boy, have we been doing a lot of detective work. So far, we've learned that Inspector Shelley is using her investigation as a ruse to discover Mummy's True Name, with the ultimate goal of using her to take over the London MLM. We've also learned that Dracula doesn't want Mummy to know about this. You're wondering why? Me too. Let's find out, shall we?

"I'm not so sure about this," Sherman said, eyeing the werewolf cub squirming in Theodora's arms.

"I am," Theodora reassured him. "Stop that, Sylvester," she said, dodging the pup's tongue, which was lapping against her cheek.

"It's just that cubs aren't great at following directions, and Sylvester—"

"Is a puppy master of chaos," Theodora interjected. She was kneeling on the floor of the Hellhound Hallway, a massive corridor filled with a vast array of art featuring canine monsters of great renown. "Who better to cause a diversion? Now, is everyone clear on the plan?"

Sylvester gave her another great slobbery lick, which Theodora took as a yes. "Sherman?"

"Yes," sighed the tarantula.

"Let's just go over it one more time: Sylvester is going to run past the Reform School classroom with the rosemary." Theodora passed the cub a bunch of dried herbs she'd nicked from the pantry. "Lessons are supposed to run for another ten minutes, but the trolls won't be able to resist going after these. Then the trolls will chase Sylvester, and Mummy will chase the trolls!"

I suppose you're wondering why Theodora was so convinced that the trolls would be lured out of class by a bunch of dried herbs? It's a fair question. The answer is that trolls find them simply irresistible: in fact, when they were first sentenced to a spell in Reform School, they had been lured to the mansion by Sir Pumpkin-de-Patch waving bunches of basil over his head. Theodora figured if it had worked for the Monster-Gardener-in-Chief, then it would work for her.

"OK, Sylvester. Ready, steady, go!" She released the cub, who took off at once. Theodora and

Sherman ducked behind a statue of a three-headed dog to wait. Five minutes later, Sylvester, still clutching the rosemary in his jaws, went bounding past. Hot on his tail was a pair of lumbering trolls (one of whom was still clutching a pamphlet, *Twelve Steps to Good Monster Behaviour*, in his oversized fist) and an exasperated Mummy.

"Give us the herbs," cried the trolls. "We're hungry!"

"For darkness' sake, you've only just had lunch!" Mummy snapped as she hurried past.

Theodora waited until their collective footsteps had faded, then popped out from behind the statue. "See, Sherman? I told you it would work. If we hurry, we might make the start of the meeting… I wonder why Dracula invited us along? We've never been allowed to attend before."

Theodora and Sherman made their way to the back of the library, where a once-grand desk (you just don't see craftsmanship like that any more) stood beneath a domed skylight. Perched upon its chipped, scratched surface were the librarians – a skull named Hamlet and a raven named Mousetrap.

"'Lo, Theodora, Sherman," said Hamlet, bone jaw clattering against the desk.

"Hi, Hamlet," said Theodora. "We're going to the mausoleum. Can you please let us in?"

The mausoleum was miles beneath the mansion, accessible only through a secret passageway strictly monitored by the librarians.

"Yes, Dracula mentioned the unusual circumstances," Hamlet said, regarding her with interest. "Mousetrap?"

At the skull's behest, the raven took flight. (It was a well-known fact that Mousetrap only took orders from Hamlet; there's a very good explanation for why this is, but not one I'm at liberty to share at this time.)

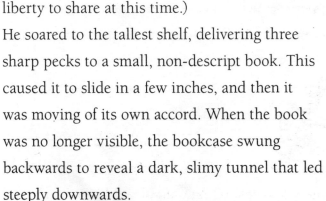

He soared to the tallest shelf, delivering three sharp pecks to a small, non-descript book. This caused it to slide in a few inches, and then it was moving of its own accord. When the book was no longer visible, the bookcase swung backwards to reveal a dark, slimy tunnel that led steeply downwards.

"Thanks," Theodora said, pulling a torch off the wall. With Sherman still perched on her shoulder, she made her way down, down, down, arriving at the mausoleum entrance to find the mismatched eyes (a star and a crescent moon, respectively) of Sir Pumpkin-de-Patch blinking at her through a slit in the door.

"Dracula said I was to let you in at once," he said, clearly curious.

"Yes," Theodora said importantly, lifting her chin.

"Hmm," the monster replied. The eyes vanished. The door creaked open as Sir Pumpkin-de-Patch stepped aside to let her pass.

A dozen monsters were scattered about the dimly lit chamber, leaning against the cracked marble tombs sprinkled about the space. A lone worktable stood in the centre, littered with bits of parchment, a couple of fountain pens and the occasional goblet. Theodora sat on its edge between Bandit, who was vigorously cleaning his paw, and Grimeny Cricket, who was pouring over a thick leather-bound tome (*The Monstrous Mash-up of Laws, Edicts and Directives*).

"Thank you all for coming at such short notice," Dracula began.

"What's this about?" asked Grimeny Cricket. "I was preparing a brief for Headquarters…"

"I'm sorry to have interrupted you, but this is urgent: we've learned that Inspector Shelley is using her investigation as a ruse to discover Mummy's True Name."

There was a moment of stunned silence.

Then: "How dare she?" the monsters exploded. "Outrageous!"

"We should notify Headquarters at once," declared Pimms the Poltergeist, who was floating upside down over a particularly old, crumbling headstone.

"They're not likely to believe us – it's her word against ours," Wilhelmina said. "Besides, if Headquarters gets involved, Mummy is bound to find out what the inspector is up to – and we can't let that happen under any circumstances."

Theodora straightened, hoping that she was about to learn why Dracula, and now Wilhelmina, did not want to inform Mummy of the inspector's plans.

"Definitely not," Marty agreed. "Not after what she did to Ork the Ogre when he was searching for her True Name."

"Or the Maaaage of Gaaalwaaaaay," sang Figaro.

"Or Barbara, that banshee from Brunswick," drooled Gabe, a ghoul.

"Wait, I've heard of Barbara of Brunswick!" Theodora exclaimed. "She was in a book I read, *Mad Banshees and the Men Who Love Them*. Are you saying Mummy defeated her and the ogre and the mage?"

"Er, correct me if I'm wrong," said Marty, scratching his whiskery chin with a long, yellowed nail. "But humans aren't supposed to be in these meetings, are they?"

"Certainly not." Grimeny Cricket frowned.

"Yes, well, as this was Theodora's discovery, I thought it best if you heard it from her directly," Dracula replied. "Theodora, why don't you tell us what happened?"

And so, Theodora relayed all that had occurred in the Ancient Curse Breaking Room once again. She was a bit nervous, speaking in front of such a large audience, but also felt rather important – this was real, official MLM business.

"The only thing I don't understand," she said as she concluded her tale, "is why Mummy's True Name is written down somewhere if she gave it to Anubis for safekeeping?"

Grimeny Cricket cleared his throat. "I can answer that. When peace was first established between monsters and humans, some monsters wanted to overturn the Monster Secrecy Act – they didn't think it was fair that monsters had to stay hidden from humans. One monster was particularly furious: Abrax, a cruel king whose empire had crumbled when, emboldened by the Act, his human subjects fled. Having lost everything, he vowed to take his revenge, not only against Headquarters but Mummy – she wrote the Act, you know."

"I didn't," said Theodora, surprised.

"Oh, yes," the cricket nodded sagely. "Anyway, Abrax kidnapped some hundred-odd humans and threatened to kill them one by one unless Mummy revealed her True Name to him."

"He wanted to know Mummy's True Name," Theodora mused, "because then he would be able to control her?"

"Exactly. If Mummy revealed her True Name to Abrax, then she would become his most powerful – if unwilling – ally in his campaign against Headquarters."

"Mummy didn't give it to him, did she?" Sherman asked, horrified.

"She did," Wilhelmina confirmed. "Well, you know Mummy – she wasn't going to let those poor people perish when it was within her power to put a stop to it."

"Of course, Headquarters couldn't have their best warrior under Abrax's thumb," Grimeny Cricket continued, "so they sent a team to, ahem, get rid of him. Knowing the end was near, Abrax is said to have inscribed Mummy's True Name somewhere – no one knows where, exactly – hoping that someone would someday discover it and use her to fulfil his ill-fated plans."

"So, Mummy doesn't know where it's written?" Sherman wanted to know.

"Sadly not," said Wilhelmina. "That's partly why she's so dedicated to her work in the Ancient Curse Breaking Room: in managing the cataloguing of artefacts, she hopes she might stumble across the object upon which her True Name is carved and destroy it once and for all – along with the threat it carries."

"And Inspector Shelley thinks Mummy's True Name is hidden somewhere in the Ancient Curse Breaking Room?" Theodora asked shrewdly.

"It would certainly explain why she's been

spending so much time in there," Grimeny Cricket replied.

"I'll take care of the inspector," Marty growled, claws extending treacherously.

"I'm not sure that would be wise," Grimeny Cricket said. "Headquarters will shut us down if anything happens to the inspector – not to mention they'll throw the lot of us in jail."

"He's right," Dracula said. "We've got to handle this carefully."

"Meow?" asked Bandit, pausing his bath. This probably meant, "What are we going to do?"

"I have an idea," said Grimeny Cricket tentatively. "A good one. What I propose is …"

Well, he might have thought this was a good idea, but Theodora wasn't so sure. Keeping track of the inspector's movements was all very well and good, but Theodora thought he was leaving a great deal to chance. Wasn't there something else they could do? Still, no one had any other proposals, and so it was agreed in the end.

I must say, I do think Theodora's right; it did seem like Grimeny Cricket's plan had the potential for a lot to go wrong. And in fact, a lot *was* about to go wrong – and not just a little wrong, like when you forget your kit on PE day and have to exercise in your uniform. I mean like when you eat too many sweets at lunch and are sick all down your front and have to spend the rest of the day in a smelly, vomit-splattered outfit – *that* sort of wrong.

The Tournament

Theodora's eyes popped open. She had slept fitfully, her dreams a kaleidoscope of shifting, unsettling images: Mummy bowing before a faceless monster wearing a crown of human bones; Inspector Shelley sitting at Dracula's desk, the handsome leather chair replaced by a glittering throne; the members of the London MLM huddled together in the darkest, dankest prisons of Transylvania…

Theodora shook her head to clear it. Abrax was dead, she told herself firmly. The inspector hadn't discovered Mummy's True Name and her monster family were safe and sound. There was no need to worry – at least, not yet.

Deciding that there was no point in trying to go

back to sleep, Theodora threw off the covers and rolled out of bed. She moseyed over to her desk, picking up her torat pack. She shuffled the deck, then selected her first card, the past. It was the same as always.

"*The Lady,*" she said with a nod.

The second card, the Present, was the same as yesterday, and the day before that, and the day before that.

"*The Magician.*"

Was it just her imagination, or did the man's hair

look a little longer, his face a little slimmer? She did not yet allow herself to consider what this might mean, but as she threw down the future card her stomach squirmed uncomfortably, as if a bunch of worms were wriggling around her gut. It, too, appeared altered.

"*The Seven of Magpies.*" The six fowls grouped at the bottom were unchanged, but the single bird at the top looked less vibrant, almost as if the ink was beginning to fade.

"This can't be good," she murmured; the last time the cards had changed it was because danger had been approaching.

And indeed it was, for unbeknownst to Theodora a terrible – no, awful – no, *grave* – danger awaited her in the Ancient Curse Breaking Room… You'll find out what soon enough. But first, we have a Chess Tournament to attend.

"Excited about the tournament?" Theodora asked Dexter, plunging her hands into a lump of clay.

They were in Art, which was always a good time for a chat. The room was filled with happy chatter – except for the last seat in the back row, where an unusually quiet Billy was bent over his desk. His brow was furrowed in concentration as he carefully moulded a lump of clay into a surprisingly realistic-looking bear.

"I'd b-be a lot more excited if we d-didn't have to wear these s-stupid uniforms," Dexter grumbled as he adjusted his tie, which featured the Appleton Primary crest (who knew the school even *had* a crest?).

"They're awful," Theodora agreed, glancing at her legs, which were encased in itchy wool tights; Ms Frumple, she was certain, had chosen the most uncomfortable – not to mention ugly – uniform she could find. "Does this look like a cat to you?"

"Erm," said Dexter, glancing at his friend's sculpture. "Sure. I c-can sort of see a c-cat."

When the bell rang half an hour later, Theodora's

statue, I am sorry to say, looked nothing like a cat
(though Dexter was too polite to point this out).

"Those of you staying for the Chess Club
Tournament please wait here," Mrs Dullson called
over the scraping of chairs and clattering of paint
pots. "Ms Frumple will be in shortly."

Theodora and Dexter remained in their seats,
along with a studious girl named Ella Vargas, whose
small, pert nose was always stuck in a book.

"You're in Chess Club, The*obora*?" Billy sneered,

noticing her still sitting there. "What a nerd. That's what happens when you hang out with dorks like *Four Eyes*," he added, deliberately knocking his rucksack against Dexter's arm as he passed.

Dexter nearly fell out of his chair, blushing furiously. Theodora, however, turned a steely gaze on Billy. "I'm not a nerd and Dexter's not a dork, but *you* are an idiot."

"Better an idiot than a weirdo," Billy called, racing from the room before she could reply.

"He's r-right, you know," Dexter said sadly. "Chess *is* sort of n-nerdy."

"No, it's not," Theodora snapped. "Chess is – well, I don't know if *cool* is the right word. But it's really great! Billy's just jealous because he doesn't know how to play – and even if he did, you'd wipe the floor with him."

"You th-think so?" Dexter asked, brightening.

"Definitely."

The classroom door swung open. In walked Justin Wong, a tall, lanky boy from Year Six, and his little sister Emily, along with a formidable-looking woman who Theodora assumed must be their grandmother. They were followed by a glamoured Mummy and a sharply dressed Mrs Adebola, her trademark gele wrapped elegantly around her head.

"N-no Dad?" Dexter asked, disappointed, as a few more parents and students shuffled into the room.

"Not yet," his mum said. "He's going to try to make it for the end."

At three-thirty on the dot, Ms Frumple appeared, calling the room to order.

"Thank you all for coming," she said, face

splitting into what Theodora imagined she thought was a gracious smile, but in her opinion made the head teacher look like a toad. Her grin faded as she caught sight of Mrs Adebola – or rather, her gele, of which Ms Frumple did not approve (wretched, wretched woman). Mrs Adebola boldly returned her stare. Theodora smiled: she knew from experience that Mrs Adebola *wasn't* someone to mess with. The head teacher must have thought so too, for she promptly dropped her gaze.

"A PTA meeting will follow the match," she said abruptly. "I strongly encourage parents and guardians to stay on, as we'll be discussing some proposed policy changes in addition to planning our annual Halloween Fair. Students, pair up and ready your boards."

Theodora and Dexter set up at their usual desk. In a twist that surprised absolutely no one, Dexter won the game in less than six moves.

"Good game," Theodora grinned, moving to sit beside Mummy as Dexter advanced to the second, third and fourth rounds until there was just Ella left to beat. Theodora was rapidly losing interest; if she found playing chess to be a bit dull, she found watching it to be downright boring. Her gaze flitted about, lingering on the window where the skele-crow (a skeletal monster which could take on the fleshy form of an animal – in this case, a crow) had perched only a few weeks ago. Theodora hadn't seen the wicked creature since Hilda had disappeared during the battle in the graveyard. She wondered, as she often did, what had become of it.

"Well done, Dexter!" Mrs Adebola cried over a clang of cheers.

Theodora's head swivelled back to the desk. "He won?" she asked over a smattering of applause. "He won!" she cried, clapping enthusiastically.

Ella walked round the desk to shake Dexter's hand. "Well done!" she said, looking genuinely pleased for him.

Dexter grinned back.

"Congratulations," Ms Frumple said woodenly,

passing Dexter a large silver trophy.

"Th-thank you," he replied. He turned to Theodora. "I thought I was going to lose in the f-final game," he said, "but I just managed to pull it off. It was s-so exciting!"

"Yeah, it was!" Theodora agreed, crossing her fingers behind her back.

"I just wish my d-dad had m-made it."

"I know, but you can show him your trophy tonight!"

"Come, Dexter," said Mrs Adebola. "I'll drop you off at home, then return for the PTA meeting. Theodora, would you like a lift?"

"Thanks, but I'm OK," said Theodora, knowing Mummy didn't want any humans around the mansion right now. "It's a quick walk. See you at home, Mummy."

"There's pizza in the fridge," she replied. "But just one slice. And, Theodora, do your homework – *all of it*. If I get one more call from Mrs Dullson saying that you've 'forgotten' your Maths homework again, you're grounded."

The Unanswerable Question

"How was the tournament?" Sherman asked as Theodora sauntered into the kitchen.

"I was out after the first round, but Dexter won the whole thing!" she said, making her way to the fridge. She took out two slices of pizza and a jar of strawberry jam.

"You're to do your homework right away," Wilhelmina called from the corner. She was bent over the cauldron, stirring a potion the exact same shade of green as mint chocolate chip ice cream (the best flavour). "Mummy's orders. Where is she, anyway?"

"Still at school," Theodora replied, popping the pizza into the mini oven. (Don't ever reheat pizza in

the microwave; it makes the crust soggy and no one
– I mean absolutely no one – likes a soggy crust.)
"There's a PTA meeting."

Wilhelmina's wooden spoon paused mid-stir.
"That's today? They're voting on who's going to host
the Halloween Fair, aren't they?"

"That's what Ms Frumple said."

"Perhaps I'll go too," Wilhelmina mused,
dropping the spoon on the butcher's block. She
swept out of the kitchen with the distinct air of a
witch on a mission.

"I wonder what that was about?" Sherman asked
as Theodora pulled the sizzling slices out of the oven.
"Wilhelmina never goes to PTA meetings. She doesn't
like how the other parents look down on Mummy."

"Who knows?" Theodora shrugged, slathering
one of the slices with strawberry jam and placing it
in front of Sherman.

"You're actually doing your homework, then?"
he asked as Theodora removed her books from her
backpack.

"Guess so," she replied through a steaming bite of pizza. "Why?"

"No reason… Only, with Mummy and Wilhelmina at the PTA meeting, and Dracula tending to the inspector, this might be a good time to do a little digging. I'd like to learn more about this True Name business. If we can discover where Mummy's True Name is written before the Inspector does—"

"Then we can destroy it, and stop her from using Mummy to take over the MLM!" Theodora finished. "What did you have in mind – the library?"

"I've already been. Hamlet didn't have anything. Apparently, it's a banned subject. I was going to ask Anubis, but there's no controlling when he wakes up – I could have been waiting for hours, if not days. Besides, I was afraid that if I did ask Anubis about True Names then he would tell Mummy, and she'd want to know where I heard about them in the first place…"

"Good call," Theodora agreed, knowing that the

other monsters did not want Mummy to find out about Inspector Shelley's plans. "So, what are we going to do?"

"I was thinking about paying Goldie a visit?"

The opportunity was too good to miss. Abandoning their pizza (a first, I can assure you), they made their way out of the kitchen, down a corridor dripping with cobweb-clad candelabras, and into the bare little room that led to Goldie's tower. It was empty except for a threadbare armchair, the Wall of Shame (on which hung the portraits of exiled monsters, including Hilda, the hag who had tried to kidnap Theodora) and three heads – yes, heads – sticking out of the wall: a ruby-eyed rabbit, a sly-looking fox and a deer with gilded antlers.

"Theodora, Sherman," said the rabbit in a reedy voice. "To what do we owe the pleasure?"

"Hello, heads. We'd like to visit Goldie."

The heads exchanged a look.

"That may not be the best idea," the rabbit said

delicately. "I'm afraid Goldie's not feeling well. She's got a bit of a fever."

"She's practically burning up," the fox added.

"We'll only be a minute," Theodora pleaded. "Besides, shouldn't someone check on her?"

"I suppose. But be quick about it."

Theodora promised that they would. She crossed the room, pressing a finger over a tiny tear in the wallpaper. The wall shivered and a small, round door appeared. She eased it open and stepped over the threshold, moving towards a spiral staircase. Up and up they went, climbing the narrow, spindly stairs until they hit what appeared to be a dead end. Then Theodora caught a glimpse of something metallic – or rather, the tail of something metallic – scraping its way down the stone tower. Without so much as a "How do you do?" the massive, scaly tail encircled Theodora's waist, hoisting her into the air.

And just who did the tail belong to? Goldie, of course!

In case you've forgotten, Goldie is a wosnak, one of the rarest, oldest creatures on earth. Wosnaks have the body of a cobra and the head of a woman. They can also grant wishes (although eternal youth and ending world hunger are, unfortunately, out of the question). In exchange, they ask for a fee: a present – an option no one ever chooses, as wosnaks are notoriously difficult to please (not unlike my ex-wife, come to think of it), or the correct answer to a riddle.

"Theodoraaaa," Goldie sighed in a voice made of rustling leaves. "Ssssherman. What do you sssseek?"

Theodora didn't answer straight away, mesmerized by Goldie's fiery eyes, burning more brightly than she'd ever seen them do. "Are you feeling OK, Goldie? The heads said you had a fever."

"It's that insssspector," Goldie spat. "Her icccce callssss to my fiiiire. Now, what do you sssseek?" she repeated.

"We seek the answer to a question, please: where is Mummy's True Name hidden?"

Goldie's eyes blazed, as if kindling had been added to their flames. Theodora and Sherman looked away; it was like staring into twin suns.

"Noooo."

Theodora blinked, nonplussed. "Is that some sort of riddle?"

"Noooo," the wosnak hissed. "I cannot ansssswer your quesssstion."

Theodora and Sherman exchanged a startled

look. Goldie had never refused one of their requests before – not even when Theodora had asked for a key to Dracula's study, or when Sherman had asked for a never-ending supply of strawberry jam.

"But—"

"Thissss issss the one topic of which I am forbidden to sssspeak. Issss there ssssomething elsssse?"

"No," Theodora said, disappointed.

At the same time, Sherman said, "Yes: what kind of monster is Inspector Shelley?"

"Good one," Theodora said, annoyed she hadn't thought to ask this herself. The more they could learn about the inspector, the better; maybe there was something she wanted even more than taking

over the MLM. If they could offer her that –
whatever that might be – then maybe the inspector
could be persuaded to abandon her plans, and she
wouldn't care to keep looking for Mummy's True
Name, let alone use it.

Goldie tilted her head, considering. "Gift or
riddddle?"

"Riddle," Sherman said confidently; he was quite
good at solving puzzles.

"Verrrry well. Riddle me thissss:

> Bold new worlds do I create,
> People you love, and love to hate.
> I reveal your deepest fears,
> Show them to you, cause your tears.
> Or I can make your hopes soar high,
> Rays of light in a bright blue sky.
> Think long and hard, don't lose the plot –
> My words, you see, are all you've got.

What am I?"

Theodora hadn't the slightest idea where to begin, but Sherman must have; she could practically hear his brain whirring away. As the minutes ticked by, Theodora began to fear that Goldie had finally managed to stump him when Sherman looked up suddenly.

"Don't lose the plot, my words, you see, are all you've got," he repeated, pincers clicking rapidly. "Someone who creates worlds and people – plots – with their words. The answer," he said, doffing his top hat so it sat at an even jauntier angle, "is an author!"

"Corrrrect," Goldie hissed, her hood flaring with pleasure.

Theodora beamed at Sherman.

"But that doesn't make any sense," he said, face falling. "Not all authors are monsters. Some are human."

"That'ssss what you thinkkkk," Goldie replied.

Before Theodora could ask what Goldie meant by this, she felt herself being lowered to the floor; their audience with the wosnak was clearly over.

"Whatever Goldie says, being an author and being a monster aren't mutually exclusive," Sherman said stubbornly.

"We must be missing something," Theodora agreed, plodding down the stairs. When she reached the bottom, she opened the door to the bare little room – and found herself face to face with none other than Ratsputin.

"What business have you here?" demanded the rat, rearing onto his back legs and placing his paws on his hips.

Theodora hesitated: the less Ratsputin knew, the better. "Just visiting Figaro," she said, with a beseeching glance at the heads not to contradict her. "You?"

"Not that it's any of your business," he replied with a flick of his scaly green tail, "but I'm reviewing the Wall of Shame. I think one or two portraits should be added in light of some recent activity... Well, I'd best report back to the inspector.

Heads," he nodded, scampering from the room.

"Thanks for not spilling the beans," Theodora said gratefully to the trio, who'd been silently observing the scene from above.

The rabbit crinkled his nose. "I can't normally abide lying, but that rat rubs me up the wrong way."

"He's up to something," wheezed the fox. "I'm sure of it."

"Me too," said Sherman.

"Me three," said Theodora, chin jutting out in a striking imitation of Mummy when she wasn't about to let anyone get in her way. "And that's why we're going to follow him."

The Beetle

"I'm not sure this is wise," Sherman said anxiously.

"You worry too much, Sherman."

"Perhaps. But you have to admit," said the tarantula as they entered the Hall of Mirrors (a fantastical corridor made entirely of – what else? – mirrors), "you do have a habit of getting into trouble. And this would be very big trouble."

"Only if we get caught. Where do you think Ratsputin's gone?"

"The rat?" asked one of Theodora's reflections. At the real Theodora's nod, the reflection said, "He was just here – looked like he was headed towards the Ancient Curse Breaking Room."

"Thanks!" Theodora shouted, hurtling down the corridor.

"How are we going to get in without him noticing?" Sherman ventured as she slowed.

Theodora had to admit, this was a good question. She bit her lip, thinking. Silently, she eased the door open just a crack. Theodora could only just make out the inspector, who was standing beneath the towering stone jaguar in the far corner of the room.

"Like this," Theodora said, pulling the door open all the way. She slipped inside, dropping into a crouch. Hugging the wall, she shuffled towards the back of the room. She paused at the corner opposite where the inspector stood, ducking behind the mammoth-tusk desk. It wasn't exactly comfortable, what with her knees pulled up by her ears, but they were well hidden and had a decent view of the entire room.

Inspector Shelley was examining a statue of a sphinx, presumably searching for Mummy's True Name. A flurry of snowflakes swirled around her, melting into a puddle at her feet. "Well?" she asked Ratsputin, without looking up.

"The Wall of Shame isn't monitored by anyone except the heads, but we won't be able to interrogate the wosnak without their say-so," Ratsputin supplied. "I was hoping to find out if they can be bribed, but the *human* was hanging about, so I'll have to try another time."

"Very good," Inspector Shelley said approvingly. "And my book?"

"The library has a copy, but it's currently checked out to the Invisible Man."

Theodora's brow furrowed. Which book were they talking about? The library had hundreds – no, thousands – of books.

"Perhaps we should order a back-up copy. I've got the original, obviously," she said, patting her pocket, "but I don't want to risk…" The inspector trailed off as the door swung open. "Mummy," she said, hastily stepping away from the sphinx. "To what do we owe the pleasure?"

Mummy clearly hadn't been expecting to find anyone in here; she froze, eyes darting between the inspector and the sphinx. "Apologies," she said slowly, "I didn't realize you were in here. Helter-Skelter mentioned that we've received a new shipment of sarcophagi, so I thought I'd take a quick look before dinner..." Her gaze flitted back to the statue. "Were you looking for something?"

"Oh, no – I was just admiring your collection," the inspector said lightly, edging further away from the sphinx. "I've actually been meaning to have a chat with you. You've done a good job with Reform School: the trolls are coming along nicely. I understand they were previously employed by the evil hag, Hilda?"

"Correct," said Mummy.

"I remember her; she wanted to throw out the MLM Charter and rule over humans… Insipid creature," she sneered. "And the skele-crow was working for her?"

"He was more like her partner. We're holding him in the dungeons until he agrees to attend Reform School, as per Headquarters' instructions."

Theodora was unpleasantly surprised to hear this most unwelcome bit of news. She hoped Marty had implemented some extra-strong security measures; there was no telling what sort of mischief that foul bird would get up to if he got out of his cell and into the mansion.

"And your work in here?" the inspector enquired, sweeping an arm to indicate the vast, glittering space that was the Ancient Curse Breaking Room.

"Going well. Only one cursed artefact has arrived in the past year. It was destroyed."

"Excellent. And have there been any beetle sightings?"

"No, thank darkness. Given the … er, *circumstances*, we've always monitored the beetle situation quite closely. We've made preparations in the event that one should appear, of course."

Theodora felt more confused than ever: what beetle situation?

"These preparations include removing the human from the mansion?"

"The huma–? Oh, Theodora! Naturally."

"Very good," the inspector replied. "Now that you're here, I'd like you to show me around the Mephistopheles Parlour. Helter-Skelter said you have the only key."

"Yes, Inspector. I'll just have to run up to my room. It's in my other wrappings."

Inspector Shelley scooped Ratsputin into her collar and followed Mummy out, their voices tailing off. Theodora crawled out from her hiding space, slumping onto the bench where she and Mummy had sat a couple of weeks earlier. She fingered the necklace they had examined together, wishing she could return to that moment, before things had got so complicated…

"Theodora?" Sherman asked tentatively, creeping down her arm. "Are you all right?"

"I'm fine," she lied, avoiding Sherman's gaze.

He peered at her over the tops of his monocles. "Are you quite sure?"

"Yes – no," she said suddenly, slamming a fist onto the desk, causing the tarantula to jump. "Mummy said if they find a beetle in the mansion, they'll throw me out!" A hateful, itchy prickling was building behind her eyes. She turned her head, not wanting Sherman to see how upset she was.

"Not for good!" he exclaimed. "Mummy just meant that if something bad happened – a beetle appearing, apparently – they have a plan to keep you safe."

"It's a bug! How much damage could a *bug* do?"

"I see your point, but—"

"And couldn't Bandit just eat it?" she added desperately.

"We must be missing something."

"We seem to be doing a lot of that lately," Theodora grumbled, staring resolutely at the amulet. And then she froze, breath catching in her chest like a butterfly snagged by a net: there was something there, etched into the back of the largest stone. Something small, but apparently dangerous. Something she couldn't fail to recognize.

A beetle.

Mummy Victorious

"Sherman," Theodora said in a hushed voice.

"I think we ought to…"

"Sherman!"

The tarantula blinked. "What?"

"Take a look at this, will you?"

Sherman crept across the desk, peering at the stone. "Oh, my. Is that a—?"

"Beetle," she confirmed.

He let out a squeak, scurrying backwards. Thankfully, Theodora caught him before he skidded off the desk. Before she could admonish him to stay calm, a booming voice asked, "Did someone say beetle?"

It was Anubis, eyes glowing, mouth smoking.

Theodora groaned inwardly. Why did Anubis have to wake up now? Wasn't it bad enough that she had just discovered a beetle – a beetle whose appearance was likely to result in her being made to leave the mansion – without getting in trouble with Anubis, too? And what if he told Mummy? She would be so disappointed that Theodora had been in the Ancient Curse Breaking Room without monster supervision – she would definitely be grounded… Maybe it was best to say nothing at all? She glanced at Sherman, who was looking at Theodora with a little too much understanding. She sighed. There was nothing for it; if she didn't tell Anubis about the beetle, then Sherman would.

"Yes," she said grudgingly. "There's a beetle etched into the back of this jewel."

"Odd," he murmured, smoke pouring out of his mouth in great green plumes. "I sensed no jinx upon it – and beetles are cursed creatures, so I should have done… And the Sight Extender didn't detect anything?"

"Nope. It turned yellow."

"Check again," intoned the statue.

Theodora plucked the Sight Extender off the desk, positioning it over the amulet. The eyeball glowed yellow, just as it had before. And then, just as it had before (unbeknownst to her), it finally flushed a vivid, angry red.

"It is cursed," Sherman said in a hushed voice.

Hands shaking slightly (yours would too if you were holding a cursed item), Theodora was about to drop the Sight Extender when the eyeball blinked again. A white-bright light shot out of the lens, hitting the necklace square in the middle of the main stone. And then the most unbelievable – no, unimaginable – no, impossible – thing happened…

The jewel split like a freshly cracked egg,

breaking in two. The stones were emitting a strange clicking sound and, most alarmingly, something was emerging from the fragments. Something small and black and shiny: a beetle – and this was no etching. No, this was the real thing. It had a hard outer shell, oversized wings and strange markings upon its metallic-blue head. Free of its glittering cage, the scarab took flight. It landed with a thud on the floor, skittering towards the exit.

"Don't let it escape!" Anubis cried.

But it was too late. The beetle was gone, having

squeezed through the narrow gap between the floor
and door.

"That beetle must be destroyed at all costs," Anubis
said urgently. "It is a symbol of the evil spirit Osiris
and those who worship him. They carry a curse that
can awaken all sorts of evils… Get Mummy. Now!"
he roared when Theodora didn't move.

Theodora jumped, snatched Sherman off the
desk, and raced from the room.

"Mummy," Theodora said breathlessly, blowing into the kitchen like a hurricane. "Mummy, I—"

"Guess what?" Mummy cut her off, cheeks flushed with excitement. "The school's just phoned – I've been chosen to host this year's Halloween Fair!" She pulled Theodora into a hug. "Can you believe it? Not a single vote of support in the past five years, and this year it was unanimous!"

"Yes," said Wilhelmina, smiling mischievously. "You did very well."

"That's great," said Theodora. "But—"

"Perfect timing, too," Wilhelmina interjected. "The inspector will be gone by then. It can double up as a celebration of her departure!"

"But what about our All Hallows' Eve celebration?" asked Helter-Skelter. "We can't very well have a bunch of humans around for the Monster Ball – we'd be breaking **Rule Number One**. Again."

"We'll just hold the parties in separate rooms," Wilhelmina said unconcernedly. "I don't even think we'll need glamours – the humans will just think we're wearing Halloween costumes!"

"It's going to be wonderful," Mummy smiled, launching into her plans for both events. "We'll serve roasted lizard legs and snake guts for the monsters, chicken satay and Swedish meatballs for the humans. We'll book two bands – I'm thinking The Phantoms Purple for the Monster Ball and Oakes and Smith for the fair. And I'll ask Marty to organize some games for both events, and…"

Theodora stood helplessly as Mummy rambled on, and on, and on. When she finally took a breath, Theodora started to explain about the beetle, but then Inspector Shelley entered the kitchen. Well, Theodora couldn't speak freely in front of her. Nor would she be able to any time soon; the inspector and Ratsputin seemed to be everywhere all at once.

"They're always hanging about," Sherman complained later, when they'd left the kitchen, having finally given up on getting Mummy to themselves. "At this rate, we'll never be able to tell Mummy about the beetle. Maybe we should talk to Dracula, or Wilhelmina."

"Maybe," Theodora said non-committally. She had no desire to tell any of the monsters about the beetle, given the chain of events it could lead to... True, Anubis had said it was cursed, but how could he possibly know that? Surely not every beetle in the whole, wide world was cursed? More likely than not, this beetle was just a normal bug that had accidentally got trapped in a shipment from Egypt. Besides, who knew if it was even still around? There was no point in getting everyone all worked up over what was probably nothing.

"Well, what are we going to do?" Sherman asked.

Theodora paused, then met the tarantula's questioning gaze head on. "We're going to catch that beetle ourselves. If it's still here, that is."

The tarantula heaved a sigh. "I was afraid you were going to say that."

Catching the beetle was easier said than done, as Theodora was at school during the day and it seemed as though Mummy or the inspector were everywhere she turned in the evenings. Sherman was doing his best, but there was only so much ground that one tarantula could cover.

Speaking of school, things weren't going so well there, either.

"Quiet down," called Mrs Dullson, calling the class to order. "Ms Frumple has informed me of some additional policy changes. Going forward, all Art and Music will be cancelled."

This announcement was met with stunned silence. Billy's mouth was actually hanging open; the only class he really enjoyed – let alone put any effort into – was Art.

"Furthermore, lunch breaks will be reduced from one hour to twenty minutes."

The effect of these words was instantaneous.

"That's not fair!" Billy exploded, leaping to his feet. "You can't even play a proper game of football in twenty minutes!"

It was rare for Theodora to see eye to eye with Billy, but at that moment she did completely; getting rid of Art and Music was one thing, shortening lunchtime was another.

"What's Frumple playing at?" she demanded.

"*Ms* Frumple," Mrs Dullson corrected. "And I believe she's simply seeking to maximize the time you spend learning, the better to prepare you for secondary school."

"But that's ages away," said a pigtailed girl named Shirley Jackson.

"And isn't recreational time just as important to our development?" asked Ella. "At least, that's what my granddad says – he's a professor."

"You should raise any concerns with your parents," Mrs Dullson called over the students' protests, "and have them call the office. The governors are voting on these measures in two weeks' time; nothing will change before then."

Theodora dropped into her chair. Billy remained standing, only returning to his seat after receiving a stern look from Mrs Dullson.

"We'll be moving to Maths," she said. "Please turn to page thirty-four in your textbooks."

A few minutes into their Maths lesson, Theodora heard someone whisper, "*Psst!*" She turned to find Shirley holding out a note to her. Theodora blinked in surprise; no one ever passed her notes. She unfolded the paper, leaning over so that Dexter could read it too. It said:

> What are we going to do about Frumple?
> Billy

Theodora and Dexter exchanged looks of surprise; they weren't exactly on friendly terms with Billy. Still, *something* had to be done, and Billy was famous at school for stirring up trouble (who could forget the time he set off the fire alarm to avoid a test, or when he put a whoopee cushion on Mrs Dullson's chair?). And Theodora figured Ms Frumple deserved a great big heap of it.

She looked at Dexter questioningly, and he gave a quick nod. She scribbled a reply beneath Billy's signature:

Meet at the far end of the
playground at 3.15 p.m.

Yes, Theodora and Dexter were going to team up with Billy, despite his bullying and nose-picking. And that wasn't the only *unusual* alliance they were about to make…

The Telegram

"I'm n-not sure about th-this," Dexter said as they made their way across the playground after school. "B-Billy's not th-the nicest guy."

"I know," Theodora agreed. "But he's better at causing trouble than anyone, and the only way Frumple's going to back off on all of these dumb changes is if we make big trouble."

"I s-suppose," Dexter agreed.

"Wasn't sure you were coming," Billy said, wiping his nose on his sleeve as they drew up beside him.

"Neither were we," Theodora admitted.

"Then why did you?"

"Because Frumple's got to be stopped," she said firmly.

"H-hear, hear," said Dexter.

Billy's eyes narrowed. "I only meant for Theodora to help. Not you, Four Eyes."

"Dexter's got a lot of great ideas. Besides, we're a team," Theodora said. "But if we're going to work together, you have to stop calling us names."

"Y-yeah," Dexter added, more bravely than he felt; Billy was a lot bigger than he was.

Billy looked as if he wanted to pummel Dexter, but one flinty glare from Theodora stopped him in his tracks. "Fiiine," he sighed, dragging out the word.

"Now," said Theodora, "what are we going to do about Frumple?"

A truly wicked grin lit up Billy's face. "I've got a plan."

So, Theodora and Dexter were teaming up with their former nemesis. Luckily, Billy and Dexter were willing to take the lead on their efforts, for which Theodora was extremely grateful – she had her hands full at home.

Inspector Shelley was still swooping about like a nosy, overgrown hawk. There was no escaping her presence, even when she wasn't actually in the room: she'd made Helter-Skelter change their diet (bye-bye, spaghetti and meatballs, hello, cabbage

and tripe), she'd re-arranged the furniture in the
Hellhound Hallway and the Beelzebub Parlour
(disposing of Mummy's red velvet curtains in the
process), and had pinned posters listing a host of
new rules all over the mansion.

"She's just as bad as Ms Frumple," Theodora
grumbled. "All these new rules – it's like she's
already taken over."

"I've never seen everyone looking so troubled,"
Sherman said in an undertone, as Figaro floated
silently past.

No breakfast
after 8:00a.m

No Running in
the hallways!

No shoes
inside the
Mansion

He was right. Theodora couldn't ever recall a time when the ghost wasn't singing. And he wasn't the only one acting strangely: Georgie hadn't picked up his guitar in weeks but was eating candyfloss at an alarming rate, Bandit was only napping for two hours a day instead of his usual ten – even Marty looked a bit peaky, his usually thick fur speckled with bald patches.

"I'm worried too," Sherman admitted, taking a bite of the brownie Theodora had smuggled out of the kitchen. (Helter-Skelter usually pretended not to notice when she was nicking goodies, but today he actually *hadn't* noticed.) "I just want things to get back to normal."

Unfortunately, things would not be getting back to normal for quite some time – at least, not according to the torat cards.

"Sherman," Theodora said, squinting at the present card, *The Magician*. "Look at this."

"Oh, my," he breathed; the magician no longer appeared to be a man. She was now a woman – and

not just any woman: a haughty-
looking woman with pointed,
rat-like features… "Unless I'm
mistaken," he said, adjusting a
monocle, "that's Inspector Shelley."

"I thought so too," Theodora
said grimly. "And did you see the
sword and the wand?"

"You mean what used to be
the sword and the wand. They've
been replaced by a book and a snake…"

"What does it mean?"

"Well, *The Magician* represents trickery," he
mused. "I suppose that makes sense, given that
Inspector Shelley is supposed to be here to inspect
us for rule-breaking, when we know she's really
here to take over the MLM."

Theodora threw down the future card in reply.
It, too, had changed: the lone bird that sat apart
from the others had all but faded. Only a faint
outline remained.

"What does this mean?"

"*The Seven of Magpies* suggests thievery… Perhaps something's going to get stolen?"

"Sherman," she said slowly. "Maybe the card is trying to tell us that Inspector Shelley is going to be successful in her quest – she's going to steal Mummy's True Name!"

"But the MLM's taken so many precautions," he fretted. "And now that Wilhelmina's cast the Scent Detection spell –" a truly magnificent bit of magic in which a minty smell hung wherever the inspector had last visited – "they'll be able to keep tabs on her—"

"Sorry to interrupt," said Mummy, appearing in the doorway. "Theodora, can you and Sherman please watch the cubs during tonight's MLM meeting?"

"No problem, Mummy."

"We agreed we'd only babysit again if we had help," Sherman admonished in a whisper.

Sherman was right to be concerned; it was, of course, bedlam.

By 8 p.m. two of the cubs were tussling on the carpet. Another was clawing his way up the pumpkin-embroidered curtains, shredding them to ribbons as he slid back down. The fourth and fifth were chewing on a shoe and a boot respectively, while the sixth (probably Sylvester – it was *always* Sylvester) was snapping his teeth at Sherman.

"Sylvester!" Theodora yelled, scooping her friend out of harm's way. "Don't ever let me catch you doing that again!"

Not remotely chastened, the cub wheezed out a laugh, scampering off to join his brothers and his sister, Lacey. (Theodora wasn't sure it was at all advisable to have so many brothers, but Lacey seemed to take it in her stride.)

I am sorry to say that things weren't going any better down in the belly of the mansion, where the monsters had gathered in the mausoleum.

"Does anyone have any updates?" Dracula asked by way of opening.

"I do," said Sir Pumpkin-de-Patch. "All Hallows' Eve is quickly approaching, and my prize-winning pumpkins need round-the-clock care. I've put a sign-up sheet next to the Charter for anyone who can take a turn."

"Why do plants need round-the-clock care?" asked Marty.

"Because we're experiencing an early frost, in case you haven't noticed, and the plants are going to die unless we do something to keep them warm. And just this morning I caught that blasted Ratsputin nibbling on one of my best pumpkins – again – and now it's ruined. Ruined, I say! Bad enough that he's been poking around, talking about all the changes he and the inspector want to make when they—" He cut off abruptly, having caught sight of Dracula, who was frantically waving his arms behind Mummy's back. Mummy, of course, was not meant to know about Inspector Shelley's plans to take over the London MLM.

There was a tense moment where nobody spoke. Mummy frowned at Sir Pumpkin-de-Patch, and had just opened her mouth to question him when Marty thankfully intervened.

"Don't get your vines in a twist, Pumpkinhead. We won't let that mangy rat eat your pumpkins – and we won't let them freeze, either. We'll all help. Right, everyone?"

"Right!" the monsters quickly agreed. Mummy, too, nodded her consent, though she still looked troubled.

"Thank you," said an abashed Sir Pumpkin-de-Patch, flushing guiltily as he shuffled back to his seat.

"Erm, yes," said Dracula, shifting uncomfortably. "Now that that's settled, Owen, would you like to share your update?"

"Yes," said Owen, the ghostly owl who headed up the MLM Post Office. "We've received a telegram from the Monster Activity and Detection Crew," he began, clamping a muddied scrap of paper in his beak.

In case you are curious, a telegram is a printed communication sent by telegraph (a system for transmitting messages). You're probably wondering

why anyone would
bother sending a
telegram when they can just pick
up the phone. It's because the members of the
Monster Activity and Detection Crew don't have
any hands, it being comprised solely of highly
intelligent cats.

Owen released the telegram, which fluttered
to the table. "It says: *Unusual monster activity at
Appleton Graveyard. Stop. A headstone belonging to one
Georgie Hendrix has been damaged. Stop. No hobgoblin
sightings in weeks. Stop.*"

"Eurg," said Georgie immediately. "Eurga eurg."

"Of course," Dracula agreed. "You should check
on your grave at once."

"Meow? Mew!" said Bandit, which probably
meant, "Can I go too? Whoever damaged Georgie's
grave might be hanging around and they could be
dangerous and if they are then Georgie might need
my help!"

"That's a good idea, Bandit. You should go too."

Bandit leapt off the table and trotted after Georgie, tail high in the air. As none of the other monsters had any updates, it was finally time for Dracula to relay the latest (but definitely not the greatest) from Headquarters. He withdrew a crumpled letter from his cape. Smoothing the parchment, he read it aloud.

The Petition

Dear Dracula,

    We are writing to inform you that we have received Inspector Shelley's report on the London MLM. While we are pleased that no further rules have been broken per se, we are alarmed to hear that the human who resides at the London MLM mansion, one Theodora Hendrix, is potentially in danger.

    According to Inspector Shelley, Theodora has free range of the mansion. The inspector is (rightfully) concerned that Theodora could have unsupervised encounters with bad monsters attending the Reform School, which could have tragic results. As you can imagine, a violation of Rule Number Two: Protect humans from bad monsters on MLM property would be disastrous for human–monster relations. In order to prevent such a tragedy (and to avoid any unwanted press), we have asked Inspector Shelley to extend her visit by one month to rectify this situation. If, at that time, her findings are not more satisfactory, we will not only overturn your Not Guilty verdict, but the London MLM will also be placed on an extended inspection for a period of twelve months, at which point Inspector Shelley's tenure would be reviewed.

Regards,

Headquarters

This was met with an outbreak of muttering, more alarmed then angry.

"The inspector can't stay on!" Wilhelmina exclaimed. "She's driving us all mad – especially me. And I can't stand that rat!"

"This really ruffles my feathers," Owen hooted in

agreement. "Checking up on us like we're naughty school children…"

"Spyiiiiiiiiing, moooooore liiiike," sang Figaro.

"It's unheard of!" cried Sir Pumpkin-de-Patch and Marty at the same time. (It's nice to know they can agree on something.)

Only Grimeny Cricket was silent. While he shared his fellow monsters' indignation at Headquarters' decision to insert itself into London MLM matters, he had realized an important implication that the others had missed: if Inspector Shelley became a permanent fixture at the London MLM, there was *no way* that Theodora would be allowed to remain in the mansion.

But there was something else bothering Grimeny Cricket too. He caught Dracula's eye across the room. "Dracula," he ventured, "was the decision to potentially assign a permanent representative from Headquarters to the London MLM brought to Monster Parliament for a vote before it was authorized, as per the usual process?"

The vampire smiled wryly, his waxy skin stretching across his skull-like face. "No – I checked."

"Curious, curious," Grimeny Cricket muttered.

The next day was an exciting one: Theodora, Dexter and Billy were officially kicking off their S.F.R.T. efforts. In case you're wondering what S.F.R.T. stands for, it's Stop Frumple's Reign of Terror. They'd taken to calling it S.F.R.T. for short, though, lest they be overheard.

"What took you so long?" Billy demanded as Theodora and Dexter arrived in the lunch hall at lunchtime, slightly out of breath.

"Dexter left the petition on his desk," Theodora panted. "We had to go back for it."

Billy rolled his eyes. "Whatever. Ready to start Phase One?"

"Definitely," Theodora agreed, glancing at a

conspicuously silent Dexter.

Dexter flushed guiltily. "It's j-just, Ms Frumple isn't going to like this…"

"That's the whole point, Four—" Billy cut off abruptly; Theodora was very strict about their no-name-calling agreement.

"W-what if we get into trouble?"

"Not this again," Billy said in disgust. "I knew he was too much of a goody-goody to help."

"We've been through this, Dexter," Theodora reminded him. "You checked all the school policies and handbooks. There's nothing that says we can't circulate a petition."

"I know, b-but—"

"It was your idea," Billy added. "I wanted to do something way more disruptive. You do want to stop Frumple, don't you?"

"Of c-course, but—"

"Then let's get petitioning," Billy interrupted. "I'll take the left side of the lunch hall, Dexter can take the right and you can take the middle, Theodora. Ready?"

"Ready!"

"R-ready…"

I am happy to report that things went very well for our young protestors – at first.

Many of the children were interested in what they had to say, and several were even willing to put their names down. By the third lunchtime, they had acquired nearly one hundred signatures. It wasn't quite a majority, but with such numbers they figured the school governors would have to at least consider their demands, which were to reinstate their old uniforms, keep Art and Music, and, most importantly, not reduce the lunch hour.

However, I am unhappy to report that they hit a bit of a roadblock on their fourth day of petitioning. And when I say a bit of a roadblock, I mean a major one.

"What's all this?"

Theodora's stomach dropped like a stone. It was Ms Frumple – of course it was – speaking in a sickly-sweet voice and wearing a simpering smile, neither of which fooled Theodora; the head teacher was clearly furious.

"It's a petition, Ms Frumple," Theodora supplied.

"A petition?" she repeated softly. "A petition for what?"

"It's a petition protesting against your proposed policy changes, ma'am."

Ms Frumple's eyebrows shot to the top of her head. "Is that so? Come with me, Ms Hendrix," she said, spinning on her heel.

Billy and Dexter opened their mouths to object, but Theodora shook her head; there was no point in all three of them getting into trouble. She followed Ms Frumple out of the lunch hall, head held high despite the hundreds of eyes upon her face, the not-so-subtle whispers filling her ears.

Ms Frumple opened the door to her office. "Sit," she ordered.

Theodora trudged inside, slumping into her usual chair while Ms Frumple walked around to the other side of her desk and primly settled into her seat.

"Explain."

"Explain what – ma'am?" she added, as the head teacher's eyes flashed dangerously.

"Explain why you are disrupting my efforts to improve this institution when I explicitly warned you that any student caught undermining me would be expelled?"

Theodora gulped; she'd known Ms Frumple wouldn't be pleased if she found out about the petition, but as they weren't technically breaking any school rules, she hadn't imagined – not for a second – that she could actually be expelled.

"There's nothing in the rule book banning petitions, ma'am. We – I – checked," Theodora hastily corrected, hoping the head teacher wouldn't notice her mistake.

Ms Frumple's gaze narrowed. "You checked, did you? We shall see," she murmured, withdrawing a copy of the *Appleton Primary School Student Handbook* from her desk. Silence stretched between them as she perused the manual. At last, Ms Frumple said, "Well, it appears we have a loophole. I thank you for pointing it out; this shall be remediated at once."

"Then I'm not expelled?" Theodora asked hopefully.

"Not today."

Theodora's shoulders sagged in relief.

"But you did ignore my instructions, and that cannot go unpunished."

Theodora straightened, heart pounding.

"As detentions don't seem to be having any effect, I think I shall have to ban you from attending the Halloween Fair."

"You can't!" she cried. "It's going to be at my house!"

"Ah, that's right," said Ms Frumple, as if she was only just remembering this, though Theodora was sure that wasn't the case. "Dear me. We can't have that. I'll just have to call your mother and tell her we'll be holding the event elsewhere."

"No! You can't," Theodora repeated, desperation tinging her voice.

"I can, and I will."

And so, she did – or at least, she tried to; as soon

as a crestfallen Theodora had exited her office,
Ms Frumple picked up the phone and dialled the
number to 13 Battington Lane. But unfortunately
for her, Mummy didn't answer her call; Wilhelmina
did. And – well, I'll let her tell it.

The Dinner Party

"The nerve of her," Wilhelmina spat,
sparks flying from her fingertips
(a sure sign of danger).
Dracula must have
thought so too, for
he took a step
back. "I agree,"
he said. "But
I must say, you
handled her very
well."

"Curses right, I did,"
Wilhelmina replied,

waving a still-blazing hand. A spark flew off, landing on Mummy's magazine (*Monster Educators' Weekly*), which, being made of paper, promptly caught fire.

Dracula hastily backed away (vampires and fire don't mix; that particular myth happens to be true), pulling his cape across his face so that only his eyes were visible. Luckily, Helter-Skelter came to his rescue, extinguishing the flames with a bucket of water.

"Thank you," Dracula murmured.

"I've got more standing by," Helter-Skelter murmured back. "I haven't seen her this wound up since the cubs used her wand as a chew toy."

"Who does she think she is?" Wilhelmina raged, oblivious to their exchange. "Theodora didn't even break any rules – for once – and that dragon still tried to punish her!"

"Tried, but failed," Dracula said with a wan smile. "You must have made a very convincing case."

"Indeed."

"Wilhelmina, Dracula, the most awful thing

has happened!" Theodora wailed, rushing into the kitchen. "Ms Frumple said I can't go to the Halloween Fair—"

"You can," Wilhelmina interrupted.

"And that Mummy can't host it any more—"

"She can, too."

"And – wait, what?"

"It's all fixed," the witch said smugly. "I wasn't about to let her take this away from Mummy. Not after what I went through to get her elect— I mean, not after she's waited so long."

"She's so excited," said Dracula, eyes growing misty. "She's had a lovely glow about her ever since it was announced that she would be hosting the Fair…"

"Yes," Wilhelmina agreed, sounding faintly amused. "Mummy looks very lovely indeed. Now, Theodora, can you please help Helter-Skelter polish the cutlery? Since her stay with us is being extended by at least a month, Inspector Shelley is going on holiday for a week – thank darkness – and we're throwing a dinner party to celebrate."

Unfortunately, the monsters would not, in fact, be getting their week-long reprieve from the inspector. The dinner party was a disaster – and I don't mean a disaster like when you beg your grandma to bake cupcakes and she forgets them in the oven until smoke fills the kitchen and the smoke alarm goes off and the cakes are reduced to charred, inedible lumps. I mean a disaster like when you "forget" to tell your dad that you got terrible marks in your Maths test and the teacher calls to arrange extra lessons and he comes storming into your room and takes away your mobile and your television and your video games and yells, "That is it!" until you work harder.

"What a mess," Theodora sighed, slipping between the covers at the end of the evening. "I never want to attend another dinner party as long as I live. I thought Mummy was going to cry."

"Sir Pumpkin-de-Patch *did* cry," Sherman said, crawling onto her pillow.

"That's because one of the cubs bit him on the head. Again."

It all started in the Beelzebub Parlour, where the monsters had gathered for a pre-dinner monster-tail.

"Good, you're all here," said Ratsputin in his oily voice, which the monsters had come to loathe. "I'm afraid Inspector Shelley won't be joining you – nor shall I, for that matter – as we still need to pack for our holiday. We'll be down at eight for dinner."

"But sharing a monster-tail before dinner is tradition!" said Mummy.

"Well, according to you, traditions – and rules, for that matter – are meant to be broken," the rat said delicately. "The human in our midst is proof of that."

"Well," Dracula said as Ratsputin departed. "That was—"

"Rude," Marty growled. "And I don't know what they have to pack, seeing as Helter-Skelter did their packing earlier."

"They're up to something," Mummy agreed. "Perhaps we should follow them…"

"Meow," said Bandit. "Mew-mew!" His yellow eyes narrowed. "Meow…" I think in this case Bandit probably meant, "I'll go. I'm small and stealthy – they won't even notice me! Besides, I don't like that rat; I wouldn't mind eating him – I mean, meeting him – in a dark, empty corridor…"

"Thank you, Bandit," said Dracula, accepting a blood-filled goblet from Helter-Skelter. "But perhaps it's better if we don't – er – consume our guests."

Bandit didn't think much of this and was about to say so when Helter-Skelter dropped a cocktail glass full of cream at his paws. Deciding this was a much more satisfying prospect than Ratsputin, the vampire-cat busied himself with licking it clean.

At eight o'clock, Theodora and the monsters, slightly cheered by an hour without the inspector and Ratsputin, ambled into the dining room. They perked up further at the sight of the table, laden with a mouthwatering array of dishes: beef tenderloin with roasted potatoes, steaming bowls of pumpkin soup and sizzling plates of double-headed prawns, meatballs and (still wiggling) worms, and the inspector's favourite: sautéed fish eyes.

They had just sat down when Inspector Shelley arrived, clutching her carpetbag in one gloved hand. Ratsputin poked his head out of her collar, sniffing

the air hopefully (even he could find nothing to criticize when it came to Helter-Skelter's excellent cooking).

"Good evening," said Dracula, rising slightly.

"I'm not sure what's good about it," the inspector snapped, dropping into an empty chair.

"She doesn't look happy," Sherman murmured into Theodora's ear.

"Not at all," Theodora agreed, trying to suppress a grin. She felt sure the inspector was in such a bad temper because she'd been unsuccessful in her quest to find Mummy's True Name. Feeling happier than she had in weeks, Theodora scooped some mashed potato onto her plate, and was about to dig in when disaster struck.

The cubs, having escaped from the playroom, bounded into the room. All six of them went straight for the inspector, attracted by the large, juicy steak she was eating. But something about her must have put them off, for when they reached her, they suddenly bared their teeth, growls rumbling in their tiny chests.

"Shoo!" said Inspector Shelley, pushing away the nearest cub.

Undeterred, the cub – Lacey – launched herself at the inspector with a howl.

"Be gone, foul beast!" she yelled, flinging the werewolf cub to the floor.

"Get your hands off her!" Marty shouted from across the table. Like the pups, his teeth were also bared (though in his case this was much more impressive).

"Keep your brats away from the inspector!"

Ratsputin countered, springing at the werewolf.

The rat never reached him; Bandit took a flying leap, colliding in mid-air with Ratsputin. They went tumbling across the table, knocking Helter-Skelter's beautiful dishes to the floor. At the same time, Sylvester jumped headfirst into the inspector's carpetbag. When he leapt back out, he was gripping a small, tattered book in his teeth.

"Give it here," Inspector Shelley snarled.

But it was too late: Sylvester, that naughty pup, had already fled.

"Someooooone catch thaaaaat cub!" sang Figaro, who'd floated into the room anticipating applause, only to be greeted by pandemonium instead. "My perfooooormance is suppooooosed to start in twooo minuuuuutes!"

"I'll get him," Theodora volunteered, jumping to her feet. She raced down the corridor, red hair streaming behind her like a cape (which was fitting, as Theodora had the rare, superhero-like power of actually being able to catch Sylvester).

"He went that way!" A suit of armour pointed as she ran past.

"Thanks!" Theodora tossed over her shoulder. "Where is he?" she asked, arriving in the library two minutes later.

"In the back," Hamlet supplied. "Mousetrap is watching him."

Theodora scurried to the back of the library,

where the raven was circling overhead. "Drop it, Sylvester!" she ordered, advancing towards the cub.

Sylvester, still clamping the book in his jaws, shook his head defiantly.

"Drop it," she repeated. "Now."

With a reluctant growl, Sylvester spat the book onto the carpet. It was coated in a thick layer of werewolf saliva.

"Gross," Theodora muttered, pinching it between her fingers so as not to get any more on her than was strictly necessary. She could only just make out the title, *Frankenstein*; the author's name was completely obscured by the spittle. A monster resembling a scarred, green-skinned man took up most of the cover. If it hadn't been for the fact that it was dripping copious amounts of spit, Theodora thought it might have looked like a very interesting story.

A shadow passed overhead. It was Mousetrap, settling on the tallest rafter.

"Thanks for your help," Theodora said. "It would have been bad if Sylvester had got into the MLM

Meeting Room again. Last time he pulled the Charter off the wall and—"

"Am I to understand," said a voice, one so cold it sent a shiver down Theodora's spine, "that a human – and a child, at that – has knowledge of MLM secrets?"

Theodora turned slowly. There, covered in soup and the still-wiggling worms, was Inspector Shelley. And she was livid.

The Vanishing Act

"Um," Theodora stammered, stalling for time. The inspector was obviously irate at the thought of her being privy to MLM information, and Theodora certainly didn't want to anger her further.

"Well?" demanded Inspector Shelley, taking a step closer. Sylvester growled as she approached.

Scrabbling for a response, Theodora was about to say that she didn't know any MLM secrets (it wasn't technically a lie – knowing a few things and being in on private MLM business wasn't the same thing) when she saw something that stopped her in her tracks. It would have stopped you in yours, too…

The inspector was changing before her very eyes,

appearing less – there was no other word for it – there. It was almost as if she were fading away… But how could that be? She wasn't a ghost or a phantom or a poltergeist. But then why was she looking so very – well, transparent? Theodora found herself wondering yet again just what kind of monster the inspector was.

"Ah, you've found them," said a silky voice from somewhere around Theodora's ankles.

She glanced down to see Ratsputin scampering across the carpet. A scratch marred one paunchy cheek, but he seemed otherwise unharmed. Theodora hoped Bandit was in as good a shape – she had a feeling Ratsputin fought dirty. Eager to check on the brave vampire-cat, she was about to take her leave when the rat spoke up.

"But why is that creature still holding your book, inspector? Shall I retrieve it?"

"Please do." The words sounded faint, falling from her lips in a swirl of white air.

Theodora frowned; unlike the rest of the mansion, the library wasn't so cold that she could see her breath when she spoke – why could she see Inspector Shelley's?

"If you please," said Ratsputin.

Theodora knelt to hand him the book but needn't have bothered – something long and thin and green was slithering towards her, rippling over the carpet: Ratsputin's snake of a tail, unfurling like a garden hose.

Now, I don't know about

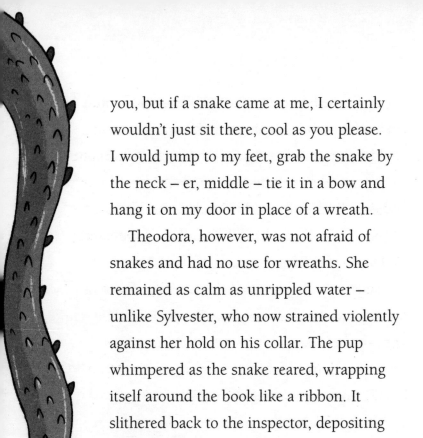

you, but if a snake came at me, I certainly wouldn't just sit there, cool as you please. I would jump to my feet, grab the snake by the neck – er, middle – tie it in a bow and hang it on my door in place of a wreath.

Theodora, however, was not afraid of snakes and had no use for wreaths. She remained as calm as unrippled water – unlike Sylvester, who now strained violently against her hold on his collar. The pup whimpered as the snake reared, wrapping itself around the book like a ribbon. It slithered back to the inspector, depositing *Frankenstein* into her outstretched hands. Her outline grew clearer at once. Within seconds, she was no longer transparent, but opaquely solid.

Unnerved, Theodora rose unsteadily to her feet, arms full of a still-whimpering Sylvester. "Erm, I guess we'll be going now."

"Be warned, human," the inspector said, a chill emanating from her narrow frame that Theodora could feel from a couple of metres away. "If you utter a single word about what you've seen, I can assure you, it will be your last. Do I make myself clear?"

"No – yes – I m-mean…" Theodora stammered. "What do you mean?"

"She means," interjected the rat, "that if you tell anyone about the inspector's – er – shift in appearance, you'll no longer be able to count yourself among the living. But perhaps the MLM would welcome you back as a ghost," he added, grinning maliciously.

Theodora gulped.

"Is everything all right?" asked Mummy, bursting into the library. Dracula was close behind, slightly out of breath.

"Not quite," said the inspector. "I'm afraid I won't be leaving for our holiday tomorrow after all."

"Oh, no!" Dracula blurted out. "Er, I mean," he said, catching Mummy's eye, "why not?"

"It seems that **Rule Number One** isn't the only law you've been breaking," Ratsputin said. "The human seems very well versed in the inner workings of the MLM."

"How so?" Mummy asked cautiously.

"She knows about the MLM Charter…"

"Naturally."

"And Reform School…"

"Of course. She needs to know that there are potentially dangerous monsters around, the inspector's said as much in her report."

"Perhaps," Inspector Shelley allowed. "But why would she need to know how to access the MLM Meeting Room – unless she's been attending meetings?"

"I have not!" Theodora cried. "I've only ever attended one—" She cut off abruptly, horrified; neither Inspector Shelley nor Mummy were meant to know about that.

"Aha! An admission of guilt!"

"Nonsense," Mummy said harshly, storm clouds

gathering in her eyes. "Theodora has never attended a MLM meeting! Right, Theodora?"

"Right," she agreed in a tiny voice, avoiding Mummy's gaze. Lying to Mummy wasn't like lying to anyone else; it made her feel a bit queasy.

"Either way, it doesn't seem that I can leave you to manage things on your own for a day, let alone a week."

At these words, Dracula and Mummy exchanged a worried look. Theodora knew what they were thinking, because it was exactly what *she* was thinking: if the inspector did not go on her holiday, then she would be at the mansion during the Halloween Fair – along with several hundred humans. And if that happened, the inspector would report them to Headquarters for breaking **Rule Number One**, and all their effort these past few weeks to keep their Not Guilty verdict intact would be wasted.

"There are more issues here than I realized – nothing I can't fix, of course," the inspector said, smiling coldly. "Send the butler to unpack. You're dismissed," she added to Theodora.

Theodora didn't dare reply, though she did think it was a bit rich to be dismissed by a guest in her home. She walked as swiftly as she could without breaking into a run. She didn't want Inspector Shelley to know that she had frightened her. And boy, had she frightened her.

Of course, this wasn't the first time Theodora had been threatened – Hilda had seen to that. But the hag's threats had been delivered in the heat of battle; the inspector's were uttered with such indifference, she might have been discussing the weather – and they were all the more terrifying for it. And she had the power to recommend that Headquarters should overturn their Not Guilty verdict...

The image of the MLM huddled together in a dark, damp cell while Inspector Shelley and Ratsputin, having put Mummy to who-knows-what despicable uses, took up residence at 13 Battington Lane, flashed across her mind. Theodora clenched her jaw; she couldn't – wouldn't – allow this to happen. She hadn't let Hilda tear her family apart, and she wasn't going to let some stuck-up ice queen and her regent rodent do so either. Not if she had anything to say about it.

And let me tell you, she had something to say about it.

Sleepless in Appleton

Before we continue our tale, I must remind you
that if you're ever in a situation where someone has
made you feel uncomfortable, you should tell your
resident grown-up or another trustworthy adult
right away. Safety first, kids!

As for Theodora, she knew she should tell
Mummy what Inspector Shelley had said, but she
also knew that if she did, she might have to leave.
After all, if a bug was enough to convince Mummy
that she needed to go, the inspector's intimidation
would certainly be. And what if the monsters liked
having her out of the house? What if they decided
she should stay out? It was too awful to contemplate.

Besides, the All Hallows' Eve celebration and the Halloween Fair were coming up, and Theodora figured it would be better to talk to Mummy after they were over. She was looking a little stressed these days; it seemed it was one thing to plan a party, but quite another to plan two.

Theodora was also feeling a bit overwhelmed: despite her best efforts, she could not forget Anubis's concerns about the beetle, which had not been spotted since it fled the Ancient Curse Breaking Room. She told herself this was a good thing; it was probably long gone by now. Little did she know that it wasn't – or that the situation would soon be coming to a head...

It was very late that night, or very early the next morning (I suppose it depends on your perspective). Theodora was restless, tossing and turning beneath the covers, picturing Mummy's expression if she were to learn that Theodora was keeping so many secrets from her: entering the Ancient Curse Breaking Room without permission, her discovery of the beetle, and Inspector Shelley's plans to take over the London MLM chief amongst them. Finally, she climbed out of bed (avoiding a snoring Sherman), thinking that a glass of warm milk might help her to fall asleep. Shivering slightly as the cool night air settled upon her skin, she crept into the hallway. And there, basking in a puddle of moonlight, was the beetle. Theodora was so shocked by the sight of the creature she had been doing her very best to forget that she simply couldn't move. And by the time she could it had vanished, swallowed up by the shadows.

Cursing her inaction, Theodora returned to her room, the glass of milk forgotten. She sat on the edge of her bed, stewing. It had to be the same beetle; it had the same strange markings, the same metallic-blue colouring. How could she have let it escape a second time?

She wouldn't, she decided. It couldn't have gone far; if she hurried, she might still be able to catch it – Anubis had said it needed to be destroyed, hadn't he?

Grabbing a torch and a thick, heavy book (*The Devious Adventures of Detective Dingle*), Theodora made her way down the marble staircase, quiet as a vampire-mouse. She slunk towards the corridor that opened into the Ancient Curse Breaking Room – something told her this would be the best place to start. It was dark and more than a little creepy, as Helter-Skelter hadn't yet lit the candelabras. Straightening her shoulders (she was not afraid of the dark, she told herself sternly), she switched on her torch.

"That's better. Now, if I were a beetle, where would I be? On the walls?" she wondered, sweeping the light over the handsome panelled

wood. "Behind a candlestick?" She rose to the tips of her toes. "Or maybe…" She trailed off, distracted by a voice that seemed to be coming through the door of the Ancient Curse Breaking Room. A soft, beguiling voice.

"Come," it hissed. "Join us…"

Theodora froze, a tingle running down her spine. Was someone in there? And if so, who? She and Mummy, and now Inspector Shelley and Ratsputin, were the only ones who ever went in there – and the voice certainly didn't sound like any of them.

"Join us," the voice repeated. "The Beetle King awaits you…"

She gave a start. The Beetle King? It couldn't be a coincidence, she thought, gripping the door handle.

Now, I don't know about you, but if I was alone in a dark, abandoned corridor and heard a

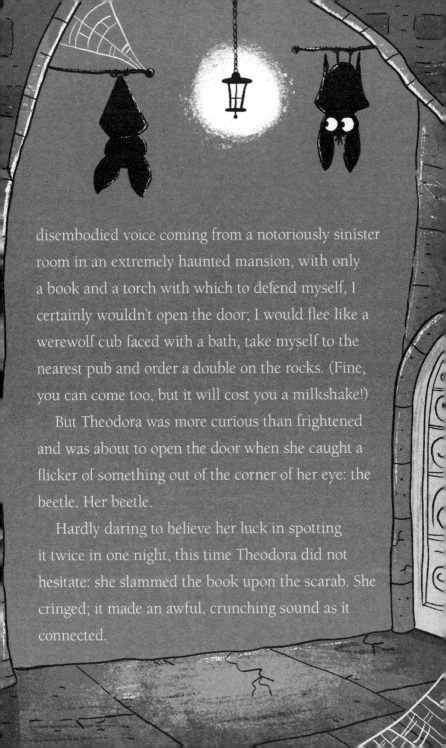

disembodied voice coming from a notoriously sinister room in an extremely haunted mansion, with only a book and a torch with which to defend myself, I certainly wouldn't open the door; I would flee like a werewolf cub faced with a bath, take myself to the nearest pub and order a double on the rocks. (Fine, you can come too, but it will cost you a milkshake!)

But Theodora was more curious than frightened and was about to open the door when she caught a flicker of something out of the corner of her eye: the beetle. Her beetle.

Hardly daring to believe her luck in spotting it twice in one night, this time Theodora did not hesitate: she slammed the book upon the scarab. She cringed; it made an awful, crunching sound as it connected.

"Gotcha!" she whispered. Feeling as if a huge weight had been lifted from her shoulders, Theodora was bending to retrieve the book when she smelled it: the unmistakable scent of mint, wafting towards her through the crack in the Ancient Curse Breaking Room door. Inspector Shelley must have passed this way very recently indeed.

Theodora shuddered. She had to get out of there – and fast. It wouldn't do for the inspector to discover her here, alone, a dead beetle at her feet. But before she could make her move, a screeching, squawking sound filled her ears.

It was Mousetrap, hurtling towards her like a black, feathery rocket.

"Shh, you'll wake the whole house!" Theodora cried.

But Mousetrap did not seem to care who he disturbed, for his earsplitting shrieks were growing louder by the second.

He cuffed her on the side of her head – hard – as he soared past.

"Ouch! What—?" She ducked as Mousetrap flapped about, swatting her repeatedly. In an effort to escape the onslaught of feathers, Theodora darted into the Hall of Reflection; so did Mousetrap. Fortunately, he calmed as soon as they entered the glittering room, casually perching on Theodora's shoulder as if he hadn't just tried to knock the stuffing out of her.

Before she could say, "What in darkness' name was that about?" Theodora saw something through the partially closed door that caused the words to die on her lips: Ratsputin.

"Well, well, well," said the rat, picking his way along the corridor and coming to stop at the book, still splayed on the carpet. "What do we have here?" His snake tail arced over his shoulder for a closer look. "There's something there," he said, nose quivering. "Something that shouldn't be. I can smell it. But what?" He shoved his little pink paws under the book, attempting to flip it over, but it was much too heavy for him to lift. "Perhaps I ought to get the inspector," he gasped, exhausted from his efforts.

Casting a final shrewd look at the book, he

scampered off. Theodora waited until the sound of his paw-steps had faded before slinking back into the corridor. Mousetrap glided ahead of her, swooping down to grab the text in his talons. With a look over his shoulder that quite clearly said, "Follow me," he flew down the hall, in the opposite direction to Ratsputin.

Theodora followed, rubbing the back of her head, where a lump was already forming. She supposed she ought to thank Mousetrap for alerting her to Ratsputin's presence. And perhaps she would – once her head stopped throbbing.

They arrived in Theodora's room some minutes later. She climbed into bed, careful to avoid squishing Sherman, who was curled on her pillow. "Thank you, Mousetrap. You saved me back there."

The raven didn't reply, nodding curtly before sailing out of the door, no doubt eager to return to the library.

Theodora settled back against her pillows. Maybe, just maybe, she could finally get some sleep now, knowing that the beetle – and the threat it carried – was dead. Sure, she still had Inspector Shelley to contend with at home and Ms Frumple to deal with at school, but that was something, at least.

Or was it?

I'm afraid that, in crushing the beetle, Theodora might have awakened something – or rather, several somethings – more dangerous than she could have ever imagined...

The Sit-In

"You're quiet today," said Dexter.

Theodora shrugged. It was break time, but she wasn't enjoying her cheesestring as much as she usually did.

"Are you n-nervous about the v-vote on Ms Frumple's proposals tomorrow?" he prodded.

"Not really."

"Well, I am. Especially since we're p-planning to protest during—"

"Shh," Theodora chastised, glancing around to make sure Mrs Dullson wasn't near by. Luckily, she wasn't. She was on the other side of the room, giving Billy a telling-off for bringing in a chocolate bar for a snack. (I honestly don't see the issue – chocolate is delightful and delicious and I encourage you to eat some whenever you get the chance.)

"Then what's b-bothering you?"

At first, Theodora didn't reply. She'd been so preoccupied with what was going on at home that she hadn't really given any thought to what was going on at school. And now that she was, she didn't quite know how to put her feelings into words. "The Halloween Fair is tomorrow…" she began.

"And?"

"And… What if no one comes?" she said, returning the cheesestring, half eaten, to her lunchbox.

"Why wouldn't p-people come?"

"No one likes me," she murmured.

"I like you."

"Except you," Theodora said with a wave of her hand. "No one ever asks me to hang out, or invites me to parties, or anything."

"You d-don't invite them, either," Dexter pointed out.

"I used to," she said ruefully. "But no one's wanted to come over since that incident with Shirley – you know, when Figaro floated into the room and she ran screaming from the house. And I wouldn't care," she added glumly, "except that Mummy will be so disappointed if no one shows up."

"You might b-be surprised," Dexter said thoughtfully. "M-maybe p-people are just too n-nervous to actually go t-to your house alone. It is a little spooky l-looking, and all those rumours about it being haunted d-don't help…"

"They're not exactly rumours."

"But I b-bet they won't be as frightened to visit in a group – especially if their parents are there."

Theodora brightened. "You really think so?"

"I do."

The rest of the morning passed quickly. Theodora felt as if she had blinked and then the bell was ringing, signalling the start of lunch.

"You ready for this?" she muttered to Dexter, straightening her hair ribbon.

"D-definitely not," he muttered back. He followed Theodora across the room to where Billy, still smarting from his dressing-down from Mrs Dullson, was waiting.

"Not gonna chicken out?" he scoffed at Dexter.

"N-no, are you?"

Theodora grinned; it was good to see Dexter standing up for himself.

"Harrumph," Billy grumbled, leading them down the student-packed corridor. He paused outside the lunch hall, where a large poster had been taped to the wall. It read: *No Students May Circulate Petitions Without the Head Teacher's Approval.*

In light of what they were about to do, Theodora couldn't help but think this was a bad omen. Dexter must have thought so too, for he looked positively green. Only Billy seemed unconcerned: he marched into the room and promptly threw himself onto the linoleum floor. Hearts hammering (they were going to be in so much trouble), Theodora and Dexter followed suit. Billy, who seemed to be rather enjoying himself, placed a hand-lettered sign at their feet.

SAVE THE ARTS!
SAVE LUNCH BREAKS!
SAY NO TO UGLY UNIFORMS!
JOIN THE PROTEST TODAY!

An intrigued hum circulated throughout the room as word of the sit-in spread. At first, Theodora feared that no one would support their efforts, but to her surprise, they were soon joined by Justin and Emily Wong and a gaggle of giggling Year Two girls.

"I can't believe this is working!" Theodora exclaimed, as two more students shuffled over.

"I can," Billy said, as Ella, book in hand, plopped down beside him. "No one in their right mind thinks it's a good idea to cut Art and lunch breaks. Frumple's going to have to listen to us now."

Soon their ranks had swollen to the point where the staff could no longer ignore their gathering. One of the dinner ladies swiftly exited the lunch hall, undoubtedly in search of Ms Frumple.

"And just what is the meaning of this?" demanded the head teacher some minutes later, as

JOIN THE

SAVE THE ARTS.

she came striding into the hall.

"It's a sit-in," said Billy boldly. "Protesting against your proposals."

"Oh?" Ms Frumple's pale, narrowed gaze slid from Billy to Dexter, settling upon Theodora. "I thought I warned you, Ms Hendrix, that any further meddling in my plans would result in your immediate expulsion?"

"Well, you didn't tell us," said Billy baldly. "And I'm leading this, not Theodora."

"I am telling you now," Ms Frumple said sharply. "Forming any sort of group to protest against this administration – whether it be by petition, or sit-in, or what have you – is prohibited in the student handbook as of last week. Disband at once, or you shall all face suspension."

SAY NO TO

Theodora's palms began to sweat; now everyone would return to their lunch tables, and Ms Frumple would present her proposals to the governors and probably get them passed, and she, Theodora, would get suspended – or worse.

But to her surprise, Justin said, "You can't suspend all of us."

"Yeah!" added one of the giggling Year Two girls, now suddenly serious.

"Is that so?" asked Ms Frumple softly, scanning the protestors. After a moment she took a step back, apparently having reached some sort of conclusion (which, based on the way her jaw had tightened, was not at all to her liking). Justin was right: there were more than 60 students gathered before her. She couldn't suspend them all – the school governors would never allow it.

"I may not be able to suspend you…" she agreed stiffly.

The students exchanged looks of glee – they had won!

"But I can certainly give you detention. One week for anyone still sitting on this floor by the time I count to three. Two weeks for anyone sitting here by the count of six. One month for anyone foolish enough to still be sitting by the time I reach ten.

"One," she began, counting on her stubby fingers. "Two. Three..."

One of the Year Two girls jumped to her feet, darting over to her usual table.

"Four. Five..."

Two more students joined her, dashing to their respective seats. But many more stayed put, and by the time Ms Frumple got to ten there were still thirty-something students huddled together on the floor.

"Detention, all of you. You will return to your seats. Now."

Feeling that they had sufficiently made their point, the students disbanded at last.

"Mr Adebola," said Ms Frumple, turning to Dexter as he rose to his feet. "This is not the sort of behaviour I'd expect from our chess champion. Won't your mother be disappointed?"

"N-no," said Dexter, his voice rather higher-pitched than usual. "I t-told her all about our plan. She said civil d-disobedience has a long and storied history in this country, and that we have every r-right to exercise it. She said sh-she was proud of me for standing up for what I believe in."

Ms Frumple opened her mouth, then promptly closed it, unable, it seemed, to find a flaw in this logic. She departed from the lunch hall without another word.

"Wow, Dexter," said Theodora. "You showed her!"

"You did," Billy agreed, looking impressed. "What's 'civil disobedience'?"

"It's when you protest against a group in power, usually the government."

"Interesting," said Billy. "Anyway, all this civil disobedience-ing is making me hungry. Let's eat."

You're wondering if the students actually got detention? I am sorry to say that they did. However, I am not sorry to say that each and every one of them told their parents and guardians exactly why they'd been given detention. And many of those parents and guardians lodged complaints with the school governors, voicing their displeasure at not only this, but at Ms Frumple's proposals, which no longer sounded enlightened but draconian. And the next day, when it was time for the school board to vote—

Wait, I'm getting ahead of myself. We'll hear about the governors' decisions, I promise. But first, we have a party – or two – to attend.

The Monster Ball

It was, as far as the monsters were concerned, the most important day of the year: All Hallows' Eve. An unholy day when the lines between the living and the dead blurred, the undead celebrating until the moon went to bed and the sun poked its sleepy head over the horizon.

Appleton was fit to bursting with pumpkins and candles and a strange, sudden preponderance of black cats. Had the residents been paying attention (they were too busy keeping an eye on their children, running from house to house in that most beloved tradition of trick-or-treating), they would have noticed that the felines were giving a wide berth to the cemetery, where a surly-looking hobgoblin with greyish-brown skin and a penchant for eating small chidren, snakes and *cats* had just been thrown – yes, thrown – out of the grave in which he'd resided for ten long years…

Of course, none of this compared to the spectacular display that was 13 Battington Lane. The path was dotted with pumpkin lanterns winking ghoulishly in the candlelight, the entrance flanked by pumpkins the size of stagecoaches. Cobwebs crawling with spiders were draped across the doorway and Fire Pixies, tiny creatures made entirely of flickering flames, lounged in the ivy that adorned the mansion's exterior walls. (You may hear grown-ups referring to them as "fairy lights", but that's just because they don't want to admit that they're monsters.) Even Bob and Sally, the gargoyles, had joined in the fun, their stone wings painted a shocking shimmering orange in honour of the occasion.

"I don't have much use for Halloween," said Mrs Next Door, gazing at the sprawling mansion as she made her way up the path. "But I must say, those decorations are impressive."

"I think they're creepy and garish," Mrs Across the Street sniffed in reply, eyeing the gargoyles. ("I'll give her 'garish'," Sally muttered. "Don't bother, mate," Bob replied. "Humans have no sense of style.")

"They're impressive *and* creepy," said Mr Down the Road, tentatively pressing on the eyeball the monsters used in place of a doorbell; unless he was much mistaken (and he sincerely hoped he was), it had just blinked.

Mummy had spared no expense – nor effort – in decorating 13 Battington Lane. Fit to burst with excitement, she had risen before the sun on the day of the parties. As the sky lightened from the inky black of night to the soft green of morning, Mummy, accompanied by the ever-attentive Helter-Skelter, had set to work. And by the time the rest of the household had risen, the mansion was nearly unrecognizable.

"You've outdone yourself, Mummy," Wilhelmina said with an appreciative glance around the Games Room, where Mummy was just putting the finishing touches to the bar.

"Thank you," Mummy replied, looking exhausted but pleased. "I do think these are lovely," she said, adjusting a pair of gleaming skulls brimming with sweets.

"They are," Wilhelmina assured her.

"Mummy," said Bon, hopping into the Games Room, "I've been watching Inspector Shelley and Ratsputin all day, as you requested – I just saw them leave the mansion. I thought you'd want to know."

"Thank you, Bon," said Mummy, looking relieved.

"However did you get the inspector to go out – and on All Hallows' Eve, no less?" Wilhelmina wondered as the bonadoo hopped back out of the room.

Mummy smiled mischievously. "Dracula arranged for them to have a private tour of the Jewel House at the Tower of London this evening – most of the Queen's jewels are monster-made, you know."

"Good, then she'll be out of our hair. Now, as I was saying, everything looks lovely – especially the Grimm Ballroom."

Indeed it did: scattered candles flickered on every surface, elephant-sized chandeliers twinkled overhead and banquet tables overflowing with platters of sweets and savouries lined the walls. The mingling scents of cinnamon and clove permeated the air, which was hazy with ghosts and phantoms swirling across the dance floor in an eerie, ethereal waltz.

As for Theodora, while she couldn't help but agree that the decorations were wonderful, she didn't find any of them nearly as magnificent as their guests.

There were the Cockabelles, a well-to-do family of cockroaches, dressed in their finest tuxedos and sequins. There was Pernille, a famously beautiful witch, surrounded by a horde of admiring warlocks. And who could ignore the rata-tat-tats, those most fashionable fashionistas?

They were impossible to miss, their cherry-red lips forming polite but insincere smiles. Their sharp eyes missed nothing behind their dark glasses as they took in the decorations, the food, the attendees, silently passing judgement on it all. The leader of

the rata-tat-tats, who by day masqueraded as the
very famous editor of an extremely famous fashion
magazine (and who shall remain nameless), was
watching the scene unfold with bored indifference
– that is, until she caught sight of the redheaded
human across the way.

Said redhead – Theodora, obviously – was
huddled in the far corner of the room, wedged
between Georgie and a plaintively meowing
Bandit (who was not so patiently waiting for the
entertainment to begin). She was shuffling her

torat deck, as she hadn't been able to perform her usual morning reading – she'd been too busy helping Mummy get her costume ready. ("Hold still, Theodora." "I can't – this material is too itchy!")

It goes without saying that the first card she selected, the past, revealed *The Lady*. And, just as they had done these past few weeks, the second and third cards she pulled from the deck revealed *The Magician* and *The Seven of Magpies*, which were not altered any further. Theodora just wished she knew what this meant.

"You must be Theodora."

She looked up so quickly she cricked her neck. "Hi," Theodora said cautiously, rubbing the back of her head; standing before her was the leader of the rata-tat-tats.

"That's a lovely torat deck," said the monster. "Very chic."

"Th-thanks," Theodora stammered. "Georgie gave it to me."

"Yes, of course," she replied, gaze sliding to

the zombie, who was enjoying a cone full of ant-flavoured candyfloss. (Ew.) "I haven't seen these in ages. I created them, you know."

"Wow," said Theodora, suitably impressed.

"Yes," the monster replied proudly. "Some of my best work. Making them was rather difficult. Well, the cards reflect the child… I suppose you must be rather difficult too."

"I am not!"

But the rata-tat-tat wasn't listening. "*The Lady* was especially challenging to compose," she added softly, grazing a well-manicured hand against the face of the card.

And then something strange happened – something very strange indeed.

At the rata-tat-tat's touch, the golden-haired woman on the card turned her head. She met the monster's calculating gaze head-on, her expression defiant. Having been distracted by the start of Figaro's performance, Theodora didn't notice any of this. And by the time she turned back to the cards, *The Lady* had resumed her usual pose, with Theodora none the wiser.

"Very challenging," the monster repeated drily. "Do take care of them." And with that she sauntered away, hips swaying in time to the wailing saws of the phantom band.

"What was that about?" Sherman wondered.

"Meow. Meoooow. Mew," said Bandit, which I think meant, "I wouldn't worry about it – rata-tat-tats are notoriously stuck-up monsters who shoo you away if you shed fur on their clothes, and I wish Mummy would stop inviting them to parties!"

"Theodora," said Helter-Skelter, appearing with a tray of smoking drinks balanced on one arm, a plate of crab cakes on the other. "Dexter's here with his parents. They're in the parlour."

"Thanks," said Theodora, jumping to her feet.

Little did she know, Dexter wasn't the only one waiting for her…

The Intruder

The Beelzebub Parlour also looked stunning: purple streamers adorned the walls, clusters of black balloons floated in the corners and a scattering of candles cast a warm orange glow across the space. A trio of ghoulish bartenders were mixing drinks in one corner, while apron-clad skeletons meandered about the room, passing out canapés.

"What are you supposed to be?" Theodora asked Dexter, his khaki shorts and shirt. A safari hat and butterfly net completed the ensemble.

"An entomologist – that's someone who studies insects. What are you?" he asked, glancing at her costume, a black T-shirt and leggings, which

Mummy had painted with glittering cobwebs. "A s-spiderweb?"

"We thought it would work well," said Sherman, "as I'll be spending the evening on Theodora's shoulder."

"Cool," Dexter said admiringly. "Anyone f-from school here yet?"

"No," admitted Theodora. "Just a few of our neighbours."

"T-they'll come. Hey, what's that?" he asked suddenly, pointing across the room.

Theodora and Sherman turned as one. Their mouths fell open as they were rendered speechless by the gross – no, disgusting – no, nauseating – sight before them.

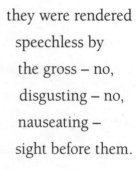

Beetles. Lots of beetles. A hissing, clicking stream of them, trickling into the room through an abandoned vampire-mousehole. They hugged the wall, flowing out into the corridor like a sickly black river.

"Oh, this is bad," Sherman moaned. "Really, really bad…"

"Where are they going?" Theodora wondered, finally finding her tongue. The beetles seemed to be moving purposefully, as if they had a specific destination in mind. "We have to follow them."

Dexter straightened his hat. "I think this is a job for an entomologist," he said, leading the way out of the parlour. The trio followed the stream of bugs, encountering half a dozen cats – members of the Monster Activity Detection Crew – along the way. They were pawing at the insects, batting them into the air and chasing them down the corridor in an effort to halt their progress.

"That's disgusting," Sherman said, as one of the amber-eyed cats chewed on a mouthful of still-wriggling beetles.

Giving a wide berth to the felines, the trio followed the trail to – where else? – the Ancient Curse Breaking Room. The scarabs were squeezing through the narrow gap between the floor and the door, vanishing into the chamber.

"Right," said Theodora, straightening her shoulders. "We're going in. Ready?"

"Um, no," said Dexter, looking at Theodora as if she was mad.

"We ought to find a responsible monster to help us," Sherman agreed.

As if he'd been summoned, Mousetrap came gliding down the hallway. He landed neatly on Theodora's available shoulder, talons squeezing her gently in greeting.

"Mousetrap! Perfect timing," said Theodora, grabbing the door handle.

"Theodora, I really think we ought to find a

responsible monster…"

"Mousetrap *is* a responsible monster."

Before Sherman could argue the point, a terrible bloodcurdling scream came through the door. It sounded like Inspector Shelley. But what was she doing here? She was supposed to be out this evening… Wondering what on earth could make the unflappable inspector shriek in such a manner, Theodora flung the door open and burst into the room.

Inspector Shelley (looking a bit, shall we say, pale) and Ratsputin were backed against the wall. A stranger – a very strange-looking stranger – loomed over them, clutching a scythe in his massive fist. It was a mummy, unlike any Theodora had ever seen: he was easily two metres tall, his bandages were filthy and bloodstained, and an amulet bearing a single beetle-shaped stone adorned his neck. He reeked of rot and decay, the scent so strong it made Theodora's eyes water.

"Theodora Hendrix," he grinned, flashing a set of blackened teeth. "Mummy's pet, come to play.

What luck! I was so hoping you would join us…
Thank you, my lovelies," he crooned to the beetles
swarming around him. "You have done well."

Theodora blinked, nonplussed. Intending to ask,
"How do you know my name?" she instead blurted
out, "Who are you?"

"Abrax, at your service," the mummy replied with
a slight bow.

"Abrax?" Theodora repeated uncertainly. There
was something familiar about the name… And then
it clicked. "But you're supposed to be dead," she said
slowly, recalling what Grimeny Cricket had said
during the emergency MLM meeting.

"What a clever little pet," he said, looking
pleased. "You're quite right: Abrax, the great Beetle
King, is dead. I'm his son, Abrax Junior. And today,
I shall avenge my father's death – and you shall lose
your mother."

And though she shuddered at the monster's
words, Theodora's voice did not shake as she said,
"You will not hurt my mummy – I won't let you!"

Abrax laughed, his voice ringing throughout the chamber. "I like your spunk!" he chortled. "I can see why Mummy keeps you around. Too bad your time together is coming to an end…"

"You can't possibly think you stand a chance against Mummy," Ratsputin said witheringly. "She's the greatest warrior the MLM has ever seen."

"Mummy *was* the greatest warrior the MLM *had* ever seen – until today. Stay where you are," he barked at Theodora and Dexter, who were edging towards the door. He made a strange clicking noise with his mouth. At the sound, the beetles surged like a wave, scuttling up the wall and onto the ceiling, effectively blocking the exit. (If you've never seen a curtain of insects, count yourself lucky; it's the ickiest thing ever.)

"As I was saying before we were so rudely interrupted," Abrax continued, turning back to Inspector Shelley, "I overheard you telling your little rodent friend that you've discovered Mummy's True Name… My father would be pleased! And I'm sure you'll agree that my need for it far outweighs your own. Tell me what it is, Inspector, or I'll destroy your precious book," he said, shifting the blade from her neck to the very same copy of *Frankenstein* that Sylvester had stolen, which was sticking out of Inspector Shelley's skirt pocket.

The inspector blanched. "You wouldn't dare."

"Wouldn't I?" he taunted. "You can't survive without it, can you? Yes, you're already fading…"

"You found Mummy's True Name?" Theodora interjected, eyes rounding in horror.

"Yes," said Inspector Shelley, clouds of cold air puffing from her mouth. "Just a few minutes ago. But I'll be damned – again – if I'll tell it to this sorry excuse for a monster."

Theodora felt a rush of gratitude towards Inspector Shelley. It was true that they would never be friends – Theodora could never forgive the inspector's attempts to take over the London MLM – but she appreciated that she was trying to protect Mummy now.

"How touching," said Abrax, his tone mocking. "You would die to save Mummy?"

"No," the inspector snarled. "But I would die to stop you from using her for whatever nefarious purpose you have in mind."

"The only one who shall die today is Abrax," hissed Ratsputin, lunging at the creature. And he wasn't the only one to do so.

As the rat's sharp little teeth connected with the mummy's arm, Mousetrap swooped down, talons swiping at his eyes. At the same time, a furry something leapt from the shadows, sinking its claws into the mummy's chest – Bandit, of course. And where Bandit went...

"Eurggggg!" Georgie roared,

stumbling into the light. He did not head towards the blur of fur and feathers and teeth, but to the sheet of scarabs filling the doorway. His jaw distended grotesquely as he began to scoop them into his mouth, swallowing them whole.

"Inspector," cried the statue of Anubis, whose spirit had most fortunately chosen that moment to appear. "Get Mummy! Now!"

The inspector nodded, twirling on the spot. She – there was no other word for it – dissolved, leaving a swirl of snowflakes in her stead.

"Where'd she go?" Dexter wondered, awestruck.

"To find Mummy, I expect," Theodora replied, not the least bit phased by the inspector's disappearance. "We have to help get her book back from Abrax."

"But, Theodora," Sherman said in a tiny voice that she could barely hear over the cries and squawks coming from across the room, where Abrax was still grappling with his trio of attackers. "If Inspector Shelley has discovered Mummy's True Name...

Well, maybe it would be for the best if the book was destroyed…"

"No," Theodora said firmly. "She's helping us – we can't betray her. We'll just have to find some other way of stopping her from using Mummy's True Name." She passed Sherman to Dexter, then strode across the room, stopping just short of the battling monsters. She wanted to help, but they were so closely entwined she feared she might accidentally injure one of the MLM if she joined in.

"Theodora," called Ratsputin urgently. "Grab the book – now!" He bit the mummy's hand, hard. As he did, beetles – real, live beetles – spurted from the wound. The mummy let out an anguished scream, and the book fell from his hands. Theodora lunged, catching it by the tips of her fingers.

"I've got it!"

But Ratsputin did not hear her; Abrax had got hold of him. The mummy pulled his arm back, throwing the rat across the room with all his might. Ratsputin hit the opposite wall with a sickening thud, then slid to the floor. He did not move.

With a squawk of rage, Mousetrap took off at once, soaring through the curtain of beetles in search of reinforcements. Bandit, not foolish enough to take on the mummy alone, streaked across the room, joining Georgie in his battle against the bugs.

Abrax, thoroughly scratched and pecked but wholly undaunted, stalked towards Theodora. She stood frozen in fear, eyes wide with horror; if Abrax could overpower a member of the MLM – though, admittedly, Ratsputin was rather a small one – then what could he do to her?

"I need the inspector to tell me Mummy's True Name; give me her book," he demanded, towering over her. "Or you won't live to read another."

"You'll have to go through both of us!"

Dexter declared, coming
to stand at his friend's side.

The mummy laughed, the sound echoing loudly
in the chamber. "What do I care if I slay two
children, instead of one?"

"*You* won't be slaying anyone," said a familiar
voice from the doorway. A voice that was harsh and
ancient and shaking with barely suppressed rage. A
voice that struck fear into the hearts of the speaker's
enemies, but which filled Theodora's with hope.
A voice that belonged to…

The Showdown

"Mummy," Abrax spat.

Mummy had broken through the curtain of beetles, still streaming into the room behind her. She stood in the doorway, her wrappings moon-bright against the black of the scarabs, an angel among demons. Mummy's sharp eyes swept across the space, coming to rest upon Theodora and Dexter, still cowering before Abrax in the middle of the room. "Are you all right?" she asked the children, hurrying over to them. "Inspector Shelley said there was trouble…"

"We're OK but I think Ratsputin might be hurt."

"The rat is dead," said Abrax, a horrible smile twisting his lips.

Mummy turned to face the intruder, gaze hardening as her eyes met his. Wordlessly, she stepped in front of the children, blocking them from view.

"But that is neither here nor there," Abrax continued. "Oh, Mummy, how I've longed for this moment."

Mummy raised an eyebrow. "You've longed for the moment when I will defeat *you*?"

"Not at all," he said lightly, running his thumb along the scythe's cruel, crescent-shaped blade. "I've longed for the moment when I will defeat you. I've been planning it for years, you know."

"Oh?" asked Mummy.

"But of course. I paid a witch to send my sarcophagus here. I had her put me into an enchanted sleep so that you wouldn't detect my presence when I arrived. I awoke one month ago. I've been biding my time ever since, waiting for the perfect moment to strike…"

It must have been Abrax's voice that she'd heard

through the door the night she crushed the beetle, Theodora realized with a jolt. To think he'd been here this whole time! She shivered; they had all been so worried about Inspector Shelley – little had they known that a much more evil (not to mention smelly) being had been lying in wait.

"And what will you do once I'm gone?" Mummy asked politely, as if they were discussing a topic as bland as toast, instead of one as significant as her impending death.

"Overthrow Headquarters and repeal the Monster Secrecy Act, of course. Just as my father wished. He believed, as I do, that monsters were meant to rule the world – not humans."

"Nonsense," Anubis, having been awakened by all the shouting, said sharply. "Monsters and humans are meant to share the earth. Mummy, I think it's time to send Abrax back to the Land of the Departed."

"Agreed," Mummy said, striding towards the back of the room. She led Abrax away from the children,

coming to a stop beside the giant stone jaguar,
which let out a great roar at their arrival. As if on
cue, Abrax raised his weapon. But it was Mummy
who made the first move, delivering two swift
punches to the creature's stomach.

He was ready for her; Abrax blocked her,
bringing the scythe down upon Mummy's
head – or at least, he would have, if she
hadn't performed a truly spectacular
series of backflips, dodging the
blows. Mummy landed in a
crouch, deftly withdrawing
a pair of bejewelled knives
from her bandages: knives
that Theodora had once
seen her use to single-
handedly dispatch
an entire army of
hobgoblins…

"He's in
for it now,"

Dexter whispered, as a steely-eyed Mummy rose to her feet.

There was a clang of metal on metal as the weapons met. Abrax's rage was palpable, growing more ferocious as Mummy evaded his blade again and again.

"Surrender, Mummy!" he roared.

"Never!" she yelled, delivering a spinning kick to his midsection.

Theodora shivered, but not because of the duel: a sudden chill had swept through the room. Inspector Shelley had returned. She did not spare the children, or the scarabs, or the clashing mummies a passing glance, but hurried to where Ratsputin lay. The inspector knelt beside the fallen rat and gently lifted him from the floor, cradling him in her arms.

Theodora turned back to the fight just in time to see a glint of silver slashing through the air towards Mummy. "Watch out!" she cried.

Her warning came too late: the scythe connected with Mummy's shoulder, sinking into her bandages. She faltered, staggering from the force of the blow. A gush of small, gold-feathered birds spouted from the wound, trickling down her arm. Brushing them aside, Mummy leapt to her feet with a bellow of rage, charging at Abrax like a bull. This time, her knives connected with his bandages. A spurt of beetles erupted from his side.

"You want to play, eh?" Abrax mocked. "All right, let's play." He clapped his hands once, twice ... six times.

At first, nothing happened. Or at least, no one realized that something had happened – no one, that is, except for Bandit. He had just swallowed one fat, juicy beetle when his entire body went rigid.

Did you know that some scientists hypothesize (that means guess, for those of you who daydream through Science) that animals can sense changes in the environment? For instance, goats have been known to flee their grazing grounds hours before a volcanic eruption. Dogs have been known to predict earthquakes – sometimes days in advance – by yelping and howling and generally acting strangely. And buffalo have been known to seek higher ground when they scent a hurricane in the air.

Why am I giving you a Science lesson at a time like this? Because Bandit, that most fearless feline, had detected such a change. Oh, it wasn't weather-related. No, what he sensed was something – perhaps many somethings – far more sinister. Somethings that had awakened when Theodora crushed that very first beetle. Somethings that had been growing increasingly restless, waiting for the son of the Beetle King to call them into service...

"Did I mention that I'm not alone here, Mummy?"

Abrax asked, grinning maliciously.

Mummy's eyes narrowed.

As if in answer to her unspoken question, there came the unmistakable sound of a lock clicking open once, twice, six times. Theodora watched, transfixed, as one, two, six sarcophagus doors swung open. And through the clouds of ancient dust came one, two ... six mummies. Each carried a lethal-looking weapon and sported a beetle-shaped amulet identical to the one Abrax wore.

"I believe you recently received a new shipment of sarcophagi from Egypt?" Abrax said. "I arranged to have them sent here – I thought you'd enjoy meeting some of my peers. Come, friends!" he called, eyes alight with mad excitement.

"This isn't possible," Mummy murmured. "Anubis hasn't given any new mummies permission to enter the Land of the Living in two years."

"Ah, but Anubis isn't the only spirit with the power to lift the veil between the Lands … the great Osiris has that power too," Abrax said.

Mummy shuddered. "If you're in the service of Osiris, then you've gone even further down the path of evil than I would have thought possible."

"I'll take that as a compliment. Now, to business: I can kill you here and now, Mummy, or I can persuade Inspector Shelley to reveal your True Name to me – oh, yes, she's found it – and then force you to help me overthrow Headquarters."

At these words, Mummy seemed to grow in stature, an indescribable power emanating from her small but mighty frame. Abrax must have felt it too, for he took an involuntary step back. Seeing this, Mummy smiled slightly. "You can try," she said, looking supremely unconcerned.

"Of course, there is a third option," Abrax continued, as if she hadn't spoken. "You could join me, Mummy. Together, we could rule the world…"

Mummy looked her nemesis straight in the eye. "Never."

Theodora's chest swelled with pride. She had never felt prouder of Mummy than she did at that very moment.

Abrax shrugged. "Have it your way. Friends," he called, motioning to the mummies. "Attack!"

Upon his orders, the creatures moved as one, feet pounding against the floor as they raced to close the distance between themselves and Mummy.

"Theodora, Dexter, run!" Mummy called over her shoulder as she rushed to meet the incoming monsters.

But Theodora did not move; she would not abandon Mummy. Instead, she looked around for some sort of weapon. There – leaning against the display case – were a few flint-tipped spears. She started towards them, Sherman clinging tight to her shoulder, only to find her path blocked by one of Abrax's cronies. The mummy's outstretched arms were reaching towards her, his dirty, bandaged fingers grazing against her neck…

"Pretty," he sneered. "Too bad you have to die…"

"Out of the way!" ordered the most unlikely of saviours: Inspector Shelley. She leapt in front of Theodora and flung out her hand. A blast of snowy air exploded from her palm, hitting the mummy square in the chest. The mummy yelped as lily-sized snowflakes laced his wrappings, travelling down his length until he was encased in an unbreakable, unmeltable shell of ice. ("He adds nothing to the decor," said Sherman waspishly.)

"Thank you," Theodora said gratefully.

"Don't mention it," gasped the inspector, who was now so transparent Theodora could see right through her. "Ever."

"Theodora, look out!" cried Sherman from Dexter's shoulder.

She turned just in time to see another mummy

looming over them, swinging a massive axe. Theodora gulped; she could really do with one of those spears right about now. Shoving the inspector's book into her pocket, she withdrew her penknife, switching it open. It was comically small in comparison to his blade, but it was all she had. She raised it just as the axe fell…

Don't close your eyes! I know it's scary, but you've got to buck up if you're going to make it in this business! What's that – you're afraid the MLM won't save Theodora in time? Well, you're right; the MLM wouldn't be coming to her rescue.

But Dexter would… "Theodora, catch!"

She whipped around to see something hurtling her way. It was the Sight Extender, soaring through the air, handle over lens. Tossing the penknife aside, Theodora dived for the instrument. She caught it just before it hit the floor. And then, as if she had meant to do it all along, she spun to her feet, pointing the Sight Extender at the monster. A radiant light shot out of the lens, striking the

mummy in the face. The creature screamed. He was
momentarily lifted off his feet, oddly illuminated,
before collapsing in a heap on the floor, dead.

"Whoa," Theodora said, staring at the Sight
Extender in awe.

"Meow?" Bandit, barely visible beneath a pile
of scarabs, cried from across the room. This

probably meant, "Can someone please lend me that instrument?"

Before Theodora could go to Bandit's aid, she was pushed aside by none other than Wilhelmina, who had just arrived on the scene. "Get back!" she yelled, slashing her wand through the air like a sword. Red-hot sparks shot from the tip, encasing the beetles in a shower of embers. They hissed and screamed as they disintegrated into piles of ash. Wilhelmina gave another slash of her wand, and a second spray of sparks landed upon what was left of Abrax's army. Their strangled cries echoed throughout the chamber as each exploded in a burst of fiery light. Wisps of singed bandage fluttered to the floor in their place; the monsters were gone, felled by Wilhelmina's prodigious magical skill.

All except one.

"No matter," Abrax said with a shrug, indifferent to the fates of his fallen comrades. "I actually prefer it this way," he added, advancing towards Mummy.

Wilhelmina raised her wand once more, but

Mummy cried: "No! He is mine."

The witch lowered her hand, pursing her lips in such a way that made Theodora certain she didn't agree but knew better than to argue. The rest of the MLM and the children fell back, forming a half-circle around the two remaining mummies. Their gazes locked. They began circling each other like two great cats, under the watchful eye of the stone jaguar.

"Your time is up, Mummy," said Abrax. "As is the MLM's, and Headquarters', and anyone who tries to prevent monsters from taking our rightful place in the world."

"I don't think so," said Mummy, lifting her chin. "Others have attempted to topple the MLM and Headquarters time and time again. They have all failed – as will you."

"You think wrong."

And then Abrax did something that, I'm sure you'll agree, was most despicable.

Ratsputin Rising

Abrax struck without warning, knocking Mummy to the floor. Theodora screamed as he lifted his scythe to deliver what she was sure would be the fatal blow. She covered her eyes – she could not bear to watch…

But Mummy was not so easily beaten; she rolled aside, evading the blade by mere centimetres. Undeterred, Abrax jabbed the butt of his weapon against Mummy's hands, pinning them to the floor. Her knives spun out of reach, sliding across the room.

A dark, twisted grin split his face as he glanced down at Mummy, still lying on the floor. "Any last words?"

"Yes: enjoy the Land of the Departed."

And with that,
Mummy leapt to her feet,
cartwheeling over to where
her knives had landed. In
one smooth motion, she
swiped them off the floor
and threw them at
Abrax. Her aim
was true:
they struck
the centre
of his
chest, one
right after
the other.
The mummy
stumbled back,
a look of surprise
flicking across his wasted face. It seemed to take
him a long time to fall. At last, he hit the floor with
a heavy, final thud.

Her expression grim, Mummy plucked her knives from the pile of dirty bandages, all that remained of Abrax, the son of the Beetle King.

"You did it!" Theodora exclaimed, throwing her arms around Mummy's waist. "You were awesome!"

"That was amazing," Dexter said admiringly.

"Thank you," said Mummy, patting Theodora's head. "But it's a shame it had to come to this."

"What do you mean?" asked Sherman.

"Abrax did not need to follow in his father's footsteps. He could have chosen another path, that of good monsters. Instead, he chose to follow the path of bad monsters, all because of some inherited prejudice against humans. The sorry result is before us," she said, nodding at the soiled remains.

"I d-don't understand," said Dexter.

Mummy smiled sadly. "Someday you will. But Theodora, what's that sticking out of your pocket?"

Theodora looked down, only then remembering that she still had the inspector's book.

"Theodora," Mummy said urgently, "tell me you didn't take Inspector Shelley's book."

"I did, but—"

At that moment a gust of wind swirled through the Ancient Curse Breaking Room, ruffling their hair and fur and feathers. Inspector Shelley, nearly translucent and cradling Ratsputin in her barely-there arms, blew past, coming to a stop in front of Anubis.

"Anubis, Keeper of the Departed," began the inspector. "You know what I would ask…"

"I do," said the spirit. "And given how valiantly Ratsputin fought, I'm inclined to grant your request. But what will you give me in exchange, Mary?"

"Anything."

Theodora was stunned to see a single tear trailing down the inspector's cheek, freezing on her icy skin.

"Very well. I shall take your knowledge of Mummy's True Name, as well as the location of where it is written. In exchange, I shall return Ratsputin to the Land of the Living."

As the statue spoke, a bird-shaped wisp of vapour – an ibis, to be exact – emerged from the inspector's head. At the same time, the smoke pouring from Anubis's mouth enveloped Ratsputin's small, still body. After a moment, the mist faded to reveal the rat's tail, restored and encased in soft, snowy linen.

His whiskers twitched. He sat up slowly, paws clasped over his furry belly. "What are you all staring at?" Ratsputin demanded, blinking at the monsters. "What happened?"

"You defeated Abrax," Dexter explained. "You and Mummy."

"Of course I did," Ratsputin replied airily, waving a little pink paw. "But why is there another human in the house? And why is the other one still holding your book, Inspector? You must get it back at once – I can barely see you any more!"

"I'll give it back," Theodora said, "if the inspector agrees to tell Headquarters that we haven't broken any more rules, and that their Not Guilty verdict should remain."

"The nerve of you!" exclaimed Ratsputin, his snakey-mummy-tail hissing in agreement. "As if Inspector Shelley – author and monster of great renown – would negotiate with the likes of you!"

"Ratsputin," Inspector Shelley intervened. "In the interest of my not vanishing completely, perhaps this is a price we should pay. What say you?"

"I don't like it," the rat said at once. "But if you think it's best…"

"I do. And in exchange," said the inspector, gaze shifting to Theodora, "you won't inform Headquarters of my – er, *accidental* – discovery and subsequent loss of Mummy's True Name."

"Or I could dispose of you here and now for your brazen rule-breaking," Mummy said, fingering her knives. "It would serve you right; you're no better than Abrax, looking to use me for your own gain. Although Headquarters would probably just send another inspector if I did, and none of us want that."

"Certainly not," Sherman murmured.

"Then it's a deal?" asked Theodora, with a tentative glance at Mummy.

"Yes," Mummy agreed, reluctantly returning her knives to her wrappings.

"Give me my book," demanded Inspector Shelley, holding out a gloved hand, "and then, devil have mercy, we shall never lay eyes upon each other again."

Theodora couldn't have agreed more, and was about to pass over the book when the full weight of what Ratsputin had said settled upon her.

As if Inspector Shelley – author and monster of great renown…

Author and monster. Was it possible that Goldie hadn't told them the whole story – was Inspector Shelley, as Sherman had long-suspected, some other kind of monster?

"Inspector," Theodora began. "Did you write this book, *Frankenstein*?"

"I did," she replied warily.

"So that's the type of monster you are – an author? You're not, well, something else, too?"

"Theodora," Mummy said, "that's a very rude question."

"Sorry, I was just curious…"

"Curiosity killed the cat," Ratsputin said nastily.

Bandit hissed, lamplight eyes fixing upon the rat. Ratsputin wisely scuttled up the inspector's arm, disappearing into her collar so that only his eyes and ears were still visible.

For a moment, Theodora thought she wasn't going to respond. But to her surprise, the inspector said, eyes glittering strangely, "I was an author. Back when I was human."

Theodora's jaw dropped; the horrible inspector had once been human?

"I'm now a living legend," explained Inspector Shelley. "I exist so long as people continue to read my works and so long as I keep a copy of this, my most famous tale, close by," she said, plucking the book out of Theodora's hands. "You see?"

Theodora didn't, and was about to say so, when Sherman asked, "And the snow?"

The corners of the inspector's mouth quirked. "What snow? Now, I've had quite enough of all of you." And with that, Inspector Shelley swept from the room and out of their lives without so much as a backward glance.

The snowflakes, still swirling in her wake, had not yet melted when Dracula, accompanied by half a dozen cats, came skidding into the room.

"Mummy, I just ran into Inspector Shelley – she's heading back to Headquarters, probably to report us. And the Monster Activity and Detection Crew have just informed me that we have a beetle infestation." He nodded at the cats. "And what are you doing in here, when you should be out there? I can't manage two parties at once, Mummy. I'm not you!"

"Come," said Mummy, taking his hand (if Theodora didn't know better, she would have sworn the vampire blushed). "I'll explain everything."

"Meow mew!" said Bandit, which I'm sure meant, "Let's go back to the party. If we're lucky, we won't have missed Figaro's whole performance!"

"Eurg," Georgie agreed, lurching after Bandit's already retreating form.

"Shall we head back to the parties too?" asked Sherman as Wilhelmina drifted out, leaving just the three of them in the room.

Theodora was about to agree when Dexter said, "N-not yet."

"Why ever not?" asked Sherman.

"Well, Anubis t-took Mummy's True Name from Inspector Shelley, and Abrax is dead, so it's safe for now. But it's s-still hidden somewhere in this room," Dexter explained, pushing his black-framed glasses up the bridge of his nose. "W-what if someone else tries to steal it?"

Theodora gasped; the thought hadn't occurred to her. "We've got to find it."

"But it could be anywhere," Sherman fretted,

glancing around the cavernous room, littered with a dizzying array of sarcophagi, weapons, artefacts and the like.

"I don't think so," said Dexter, a grin spreading across his face. "I've been mulling it over for a while now. I think I know exactly where it is."

Appleton Primary
Board of Education,
Ruling Number Seventy-One

"How could you possibly know that?" asked Sherman, peering closely at Dexter.

"Follow me," he replied, making his way to the back of the room. He paused in front of an empty sarcophagus – the very sarcophagus in which the children had once hidden. "M-most of these c-coffins h-had mummies in them, didn't they?"

"Obviously," Theodora said, eyeing the remains of the monsters, now turning to dust.

"So why did you c-choose this one for us to hide in – how'd you know it would be empty?"

She frowned. "It's always empty."

"Ah, I think I see what you're getting at, Dexter," said Sherman, adjusting a monocle.

"Well, I don't," Theodora said bluntly.

"The only sarcophagus that's always empty is this sarcophagus. Mummy's sarcophagus."

"I know it's Mummy's, but – wait, are you saying that you think the Beetle King etched Mummy's True Name into her own sarcophagus? And it hasn't been discovered – until today, that is – because it's been unoccupied?"

"Yes," Dexter said simply. "Th-think about it: if the B-Beetle King had inscribed Mummy's True Name s-somewhere else – say on a necklace, or a s-statue – it would have been impossible to t-track down. What if it was moved, or destroyed? But Mummy w-wouldn't let anything h-happen to her own sarcophagus, even if she h-hasn't used it in three thousand years."

Theodora was unconvinced.

Seeing her expression, Dexter added, "Of course,

there's an easy w-way to find out if I'm right." He pulled the sarcophagus door open, running his hands along the sides of the casket. "I thought I f-felt something when we were h-hiding in here. Ah-ha! See this?" He pointed to a small, penny-sized spot in one wall of the coffin. "This p-patch is p-paler than the rest, and it's raised. I don't think it's p-part of the original structure."

Theodora brushed her fingertips against it. Dexter was right: it was raised. And there, etched

into the plaster, small but as plain as the text on this page, was Mummy's True Name...

Wait, you don't actually think I'm going to tell it to you, do you? Please – you know better than that! Besides, I couldn't if I wanted to; I can't read hieroglyphics.

"Dexter, you're a genius," Theodora said, throwing an arm around his narrow shoulders.

"N-no, I'm not," Dexter stammered, though he looked pleased all the same.

"You are rather brilliant," said Sherman. "Now can we go to the parties?"

"Not until we erase Mummy's True Name once and for all," said Theodora, retrieving her penknife from the floor.

"Well done!" cried Anubis, who'd been watching from his perch on the desk.

Theodora attacked the etching, slashing the tiny blade over the symbols again and again until they were no longer visible. As she worked, Theodora felt the tension from the last few weeks leaving her body.

Her shoulders relaxed, her brows unfurrowed: they would never have to worry about someone trying to use Mummy's True Name against her ever again. She'd just erased the very last glyph when the door to the Ancient Curse Breaking Room flew open. Again.

"There you are, Theodora!" Bon called from the doorway. "Helter-Skelter sent me to find you – there are some people waiting for you upstairs."

The bonadoo led them into the Beelzebub Parlour. Theodora stopped short at the entrance, floored by the sight before her:

The room was packed with people: a mix of parents, teachers and students from Theodora's school were milling about the space, sipping from smoking goblets. Mrs Next Door was dancing with Mr Down the Road (it wasn't a pretty sight) while a bartender was mixing Mrs Across the Street a drink. And there, huddled around a table laden with all sorts of goodies, was Theodora's entire class (including Shirley, looking absolutely terrified at finding herself back in the mansion). They were costumed as ghosts and vampires and zombies, not knowing that the very creatures they were pretending to be roamed amongst them. Standing at the front of the group was Billy, dressed as a one-eyed pirate and grinning from ear to ear.

"There you are – finally!" he exclaimed. "Guess what? We did it!" he crowed, racing over to Dexter and Theodora. He pulled Theodora into a hug, then clapped Dexter on the back (perhaps a bit harder than was strictly necessary). "The school governors voted against Frumple's proposals! The only thing we lost on was the uniforms – the governors felt we should keep them, given they're already paid for. And they said anyone who participated in the sit-in is excused from detention!"

The class erupted into cheers.

"Yes, yes," said a low voice, which somehow managed to break through the hooting and hollering. The students fell silent, quivering beneath Ms Frumple's narrowed gaze. Her bloodshot eyes swept across their faces, settling upon Theodora's. "You may have won the battle, Ms Hendrix – and you, Mr Adebola, and you, Mr Ellis. But I can assure you," she said, voice dropping to a whisper, "I shall win the war."

Before any of them could reply, Mrs Adebola appeared at the head teacher's side. "Did you hear the good news, Dexter? Your protests were successful!"

Ms Frumple shot the students one last malevolent look before storming to the other end of the parlour, where a group of teachers were enjoying a plate of Helter-Skelters delicious canapés.

"We're very proud of you," said a voice that was deep and warm and melodic all at once.

"Dad!" Dexter exclaimed, lighting up like a city skyline. "You're h-here! And th-thanks! B-Billy and Theodora helped too."

"Hello, Billy. Hi, Theodora," said Dexter's dad, smiling broadly. He had the same high cheekbones and weedy frame as his son, though he was a great deal taller. "I've heard so much about you. It's nice to finally meet you."

"You too," Theodora grinned, shaking his hand.

Mr Adebola jumped back suddenly. "Is that a tarantula on your shoulder?"

"H-his name is Sherman," Dexter said. "He's really c-cool."

"Very," said Mr Adebola, eyeing the arachnid – inexplicably wearing a top hat – in such a way that Theodora was sure he didn't share his son's enthusiasm for bugs. "And these must be your parents," he added, greeting Dracula and Mummy warmly. "What an – er – interesting home you have," he said, gesturing to the room. And while Mr Adebola didn't share Dexter's interest in insects, he did share his keen observation skills, for he said, "But what's that?"

Theodora followed his gaze to Mummy's shoulder, where a lone golden bird was blossoming from her still-healing wound. Mummy's eyes widened as the bird (most unhelpfully) took flight, landing on the edge of Mr Adebola's glass.

"Er," said Dracula, at an utter loss for words.

Theodora and Dexter exchanged frantic looks; this was bad. How would they explain away the bird, now pecking its beak into his dad's water? Mrs Adebola was staring at it, open-mouthed. Her deep brown eyes were darting back and forth between the bird, Mummy and the room. Theodora had the impression that she was doing some very quick thinking. She looked up suddenly, smiling widely. "What a marvellous trick! However did you manage it?"

Relief flooded Mummy's face. "My sister, Wilhelmina, is quite good with costumes."

"I'll say," said Mr Adebola, raising his eyebrows in disbelief as the bird flitted away.

"Er, shall we grab a drink?" asked Dracula, thinking that a distraction was in order.

Mr Adebola, still looking rather shaken, gladly allowed Dracula to lead him over to the bar.

"Hello," said Mrs Dullson, appearing at Mummy's side. "I just wanted to congratulate you on throwing a fabulous fair. You've done an excellent job."

"It's wonderful," gushed Mrs Stepford, the head of the PTA. "The food, the costumes, everything! We do hope you'll consider hosting the event next year, too."

"Th-thank you," Mummy stammered, flushing with pleasure. "I would be delighted."

"Did you hear that?" Theodora asked, slipping her hand into Mummy's. "They think it's the best Halloween Fair ever!"

"Theodora, Dexter, what are you doing over there?" Billy called from across the room. "Come and dance!"

Dexter scrambled to join them, but Theodora hung back, still clinging to Mummy's hand. Despite all the incredible events of the last hour – the discovery and subsequent defeat of Abrax and his small (but terrifying) army of mummies; Inspector Shelley's departure and promise not to overturn their Not Guilty verdict; their discovery and erasure of Mummy's True Name – this was, perhaps, the most surprising. Theodora couldn't remember the last time her classmates had asked her to join them in anything. Truthfully, she was a little reluctant to do so now. What if she messed up, and everyone started pretending she didn't exist again once they were back at school? That would be even worse than if they had just continued to ignore her in the first place.

Mummy, sensing her hesitation, said quietly, so that only Theodora could hear, "Go on. Your friends are waiting for you."

"They're not my friends," Theodora whispered back.

Mummy gave her hand a squeeze. "Maybe they can be, if you give them a chance."

"Mummy's right," said Sherman, patting her lightly. "Sometimes you've just got to put yourself out there."

"But what if—"

"Theodora," said Sherman, his tone unusually stern. "Mummy said to go over there – and you don't mess with Mummy. I mean, did you see those moves?"

They were right, Theodora thought. She took a deep breath, straightened her hair ribbon and made her way over to her classmates. To her surprise, Ella, her face painted green, a tall black hat sitting atop her head (the resemblance to Wilhelmina was uncanny), pulled Theodora into the centre of the group, squealing in admiration when she spotted Sherman.

"Here you go," said Helter-Skelter, passing her a fizzy drink.

"That butler's costume is so cool," Theodora heard Justin say from somewhere behind. "I wonder how he made himself look like a real skeleton?"

Helter-Skelter winked at Theodora (or at least, he would have, if he still had eyeballs), chuckling under his breath.

"Oh, my Aunt Wilhelmina is good with costumes," Theodora replied, returning Helter-Skelter's wink.

I am pleased to report that Theodora had a wonderful evening, as did her teachers and her classmates and their parents – even Mrs Across the Street seemed to be enjoying herself. (Everyone, in short, except Ms Frumple.) And on the other side of the mansion, the MLM and all their guests were having an equally fabulous time in the Grimm Ballroom. On her way out, the leader of the rata-tat-tats declared it to be "a monstrously dazzling affair", to Mummy's great delight.

And that, dear friends, is the end of our tale.

Or is it?

EPILOGUE

Cases Opened and Closed ... and Opened

Thirteen Battington Lane was unusually quiet the next day, its residents basking in the success of two fantastic parties. The rest of the village, though, seemed to have come alive: the chill that had settled upon Appleton had vanished as suddenly as it had arrived. The trees resumed their normal autumnal course, their fleecy leaves changing overnight from green to gold, while the flowers enjoyed their final bloom of the season. Yes, all was well in the village.

That isn't to say that all would remain well: the torat cards were still behaving oddly. While *The Magician* card had reverted to its usual state, *The Seven of Magpies* had not: the lone bird had not reappeared, its faded outline only just visible. Theodora didn't know what to make of it. (Frankly, neither do I.) Another mystery to be solved!

Now, before we part, there are just a few more loose ends that need tying up.

At the beginning of our tale, I said we were building a case. And so we did! It was my business card that Dracula pulled from his desk; it was me he called before the emergency MLM meeting. He hired me – and you – to gather evidence of Inspector Shelley's attempts to steal Mummy's True Name. Not that he needed us in the end – Theodora saw to that. (And I'd just finished my report. All that work, wasted!)

Then there's the issue of Headquarters' increasing involvement in MLM matters. (You haven't forgotten about that, too, have you? Tsk, tsk. As a Junior Agent, you're going to have to start paying closer attention. That's right, you've been promoted – congratulations!)

I hope you noticed that Grimeny Cricket was conspicuously absent from the latter half of our story? Good – at least you're paying attention to something. There is, of course, a very good explanation for this.

Grimeny Cricket has been toiling away, building his own case against Headquarters. He was concerned – deeply concerned – that they had tried to assign a permanent representative to the London MLM without going through the proper channels. Well, his brief caught the attention of Monster Parliament in the UK (who should have been given the option to vote on Headquarters' motion in the first place) and Monster Congress in the US, and even the Monster Monarchy of Morocco, all of whom were equally alarmed by Headquarters' actions, and all of whom wanted to learn more about what had passed. As such, Grimeny Cricket has agreed to present his findings at – where else? – the Monster United Nations.

That's right: pack your bags, people! We're going to

the Empire City, the City That Never Sleeps, the Big Pumpkin: New York City.

Just do me one teensy, tiny favour: don't tell your parents. Or your teachers. Or your crazy football coach. They'll try to talk you out of it. They'll say it's too dangerous. But sometimes, a bit of danger is worth the risk – just look at what Theodora and Dexter and even Billy have achieved in the face of danger. (Ms Frumple, as you know, is as dangerous as any monster.) And I'll be with you every step of the way. We'll have an amazing – no, incredible – no, splendid – time!

Unless the Shadow Mongers catch us, that is. But don't worry; the odds of that are – well, not slim, exactly. But we've got a better chance of evading them than most! Besides, what's life without a little adventure? Boring, that's what.

So, got a passport?

ACKNOWLEDGEMENTS

First and foremost, thanks to my superstar agent, Chloe Seager, for your business savvy, support and friendship – I'm so grateful to have you in my corner!

To the entire team at Walker Books: you are remarkable – no, amazing – no, *incredible*. Special thanks to my fantastic editor, Emma Lidbury, for your sharp eye for plot, your thoughtful suggestions and your exceptional patience; this book wouldn't have been the same without you. To Chloé Tartinville for the beautiful design, Rebecca Oram for the great publicity, and Karen Coeman for enthusiastically bringing Theodora's story to other parts of the world. Thank you, all.

Huge thanks to Chris Jevons, illustrator extraordinaire, for bringing the visions in my head to life so brilliantly. My friend, your talent astounds me.

To my lovely, wonderful friends, for cheering me on every step of the way and for shouting about my books: I owe you all many, many drinks. Special thanks to Sylwia Tyburska, without whose assistance this book would have taken significantly longer to write.

Thanks to my wacky and loving family, whose antics have provided me with enough material for several lifetimes (I'm looking at you, Tappy Jordan, and *you*, Joseph Chilelli). Special thanks to my first and biggest fan, my mother, Tamara Kopy Chilelli, my beloved grandparents, Russell and Barbara Kopyscianski, and my lovely in-laws, Peter and Tracie Coletto. And, of course, massive thanks to my husband, Todd Coletto: you are the light of my life, and I couldn't have gotten through this past year – let alone written this book – without you.

And finally, to my fabulous readers: thank you for joining Theodora on her adventures. You guys rock!

Jordan Kopy is a born and raised New Yorker who resides in London with her husband and poorly behaved (but lovable) cat. A financial services professional by day, she spends her nights with ghouls, witches and the occasional evil hag. *Theodora Hendrix and the Curious Case of the Cursed Beetle* is Jordan's second book for children, sequel to the hugely popular *Theodora Hendrix and the Monstrous League of Monsters*. Jordan is currently writing the third book in the Theodora Hendrix series.

Chris Jevons loved drawing from an early age, inspired by Saturday morning cartoons and Disney animated features. After studying art, design and animation at university, Chris worked as a graphic designer and a 2D animator before pursuing a career in children's publishing. Chris illustrates picture books and fiction for a variety of publishers and lives and works in Harrogate.